Imperfections

by

Lynda Durrant

Clarion Books
New York

To my mother

Clarion Books
an imprint of Houghton Mifflin Harcourt Publishing Company
215 Park Avenue South
New York, NY 10003
Copyright © 2008 by Lynda Durrant

The text was set in 12-point Bembo.

www.clarionbooks.com

Printed in the U.S.A.

Library-of-Congress Cataloging-in-Publication Data
Durrant, Lynda, 1956–
Imperfections / by Lynda Durrant.
p. cm.
Summary: In 1862 Pleasant Hill, Kentucky, fourteen-year-old Rosemary Elizabeth
strives to fit in with the Shaker sisters of this "Heaven on Earth," but yearns to
be reunited with her mother and siblings from whom she was separated when
they sought refuge from her abusive father. Includes facts about Shakers and
Morgan's Raiders.
Includes bibliographical references.
ISBN: 978-0-547-00357-3
1. Shakers—Fiction. [1. Brothers and sisters—Fiction. 2. Community life—
Kentucky—Fiction. 3. Abandoned children—Fiction. 4. United States—History—
Civil War, 1861–1865—Fiction. 5. Pleasant Hill (Ky.)—History—19th century—
Fiction.] I. Title.
PZ7.D93428 Imp 2008
[Fic]—dc22
2008023533

MP   10   9   8   7   6   5   4   3   2   1

Contents

Leaving the World's People

February 28, 1862

"**W**hen will we see home again, Rosemary Elizabeth?" Isaac's question pipes through the half-light of dawn, and not for the first time, either.

I'm about to say "Stop asking me what I can't answer" when the oxcart's right axle dips into a rut on the Harrodsburg Pike. Ma dips with it, as yielding as a rag doll. Baby Anne, in her arms, wakes with a wail.

"Hush, now," Ma says. She shifts Baby Anne to her left arm. Baby Anne doesn't stop wailing. Except for my sister's cries and the squeaky axle, all is absolutely silent.

The sunrise sheds reddish light on Ma's sad, bruised face.

Mr. Godfrey is fetching us up the Harrodsburg Pike to Pleasant Hill. We're to find refuge there among the Shakers. The Shakertowns in New York, New England, Kentucky, and Ohio take in all comers, or so we've heard.

Mr. Godfrey told us the Shaker village of Pleasant Hill has been in Kentucky since before the War of 1812. That's two wars ago, I reckon. Maybe more.

"I don't know when we'll see home again, Isaac," I say. Maybe we'll never see Pa again, and at this moment that feels like a blessing.

"We left Lucy and her kittens." Isaac turns toward Ma, his eyes as sad as hers. "Can we please go back for Lucy and her kittens?"

"Don't you worry about Lucy and her kittens, Isaac," Mr. Godfrey replies. "As soon as I've taken my butter, milk, and cheese into Lexington, I'll go to your place and fetch them. They'll be warm in my main barn, and there're lots of mice. They'll do just fine."

"Thank you, Mr. Godfrey," Ma says softly.

"You're well rid of him," Mr. Godfrey says, softer still, although not so soft that I don't hear him. He leans toward Ma. She says nothing.

"From the frying pan into the fire, in my opinion," Mr. Godfrey continues with a frown. "The Shakers believe in separateness, Mrs. Lipking. Wife separated from husband, sister separated from brother, mother separated from child. Any fool can see that's not God's plan. Mark my words: Those Shakers won't last another generation."

"Ma, I'll be separated from you?" Isaac's eyes turn bright in panic.

"Nonsense, Isaac." Ma cups my brother's face with her left hand. "We'll be together and safe, every day for the rest of our lives." She draws Baby Anne closer to her as the early-spring wind blows cold over the Harrodsburg Pike.

"Ma, you'll be separated from Pa?" I ask softly. "The Shakers will keep us safe?"

Ma doesn't answer.

We ride in silence. I think my own thoughts, as does everyone else, I reckon. I think about Lucy, our sleek black cat, and her fuzzy kittens.

Every morning I'd pour some of Mr. Godfrey's new milk into an old pie tin. When I approached her, Lucy would lift her head. As her purring kittens kneaded her belly, Lucy licked the new milk daintily. Mr. Godfrey is a kind man, but he will never think to give Lucy new milk still warm from the cow, as we did.

In the weak winter sunshine, northeast Kentucky's hills and dales rise and fall before us. As far into the distance as I can see, each blue hill is a shade lighter than the one before it. Ma once told me there's a Cherokee word for that: *cataloochee*. It means unfolding hills, hollows, and mountains, the last one dissolving into sky.

Sloping pastureland on both sides of the Harrodsburg Pike is chock-a-block with cows and horses. Foals and calves cleave to their mothers just as we cleave to Ma.

I don't remember a time when I didn't know about the Pleasant Hill Shakers. They sell brooms, packages of seeds, furniture, applesauce, wooden rakes, lemonade syrup, butter and cheese, homespun cloth, shawls, bonnets, and yarn. Their medicinal herb remedies actually cure a body. Everything Shaker is finely made. Everything Shaker is of the highest quality.

Everything Shaker is perfect. Or so Mrs. Godfrey says.

Mr. Godfrey gives the reins a shake. His horse doesn't break stride as we ascend over a hill. "There's confession, communality, and celibacy—known as the three Cs. Men and women live on opposite sides of everything, like a monastery. Popery right here in northern Kentucky! And they shake as they worship. They quake like beech leaves in a high wind. They roll on the floor. They shriek and holler out their own songs. And all at once, too."

He winces. "The pagan and the Popish—from the frying pan into the fire, if you ask me."

Ma straightens up and shifts Baby Anne to her right arm again. I can almost hear her saying "Nobody asked you." Baby Anne whimpers. Finally, the rocking of the oxcart lulls her to sleep.

The three Cs, I think. *Confession, communality, and celibacy. All I can think about now is a safe place to live. I'll worry about all that later.*

It's late morning when we reach Pleasant Hill. We pass through a whitewashed gate with well-tended whitewashed double fencing all round. You can always tell the quality of a farm by the quality of its fence; every Kentuckian knows that. This one is a plain and simple split rail, with not a weed in sight underneath the rails or around the fence posts.

In the Shaker pastures, fat short-horned cattle, horses, and sheep safely graze. The fields abound with livestock; each mother has a healthy calf, foal, or lamb, sometimes twins.

Pleasant Hill looks placid, peaceful, and safe. *Living here will be good for the Lipkings,* I think. *Pa will never think to look for us here.*

Mr. Godfrey calls out to the first person we see, "Where to take a new family, ma'am?"

The woman, dressed all in white, walks on without glancing in his direction. She doesn't even break her stride.

"Separate, Mr. Godfrey, separate," Ma says. She hands Baby Anne to me, leaps off the wagon, and calls out, "We've come to Pleasant Hill to seek refuge, ma'am—myself and my three children."

The woman immediately stops and turns to face her. "Yea. You'll need to go to the Trustee's Office; it's that brick building on the right of the lane, next to the Ministry Workshop. Welcome to Sinai's Holy Plain. Welcome to Heaven on Earth."

With a grunt, Mr. Godfrey helps Ma climb back into the oxcart. "From the frying pan into the fire," he repeats. "I won't leave Pleasant Hill until I'm sure you're safe."

The Trustee's Office is a large brick building, as plain as unbuttered brown bread except for above the double doors. The narrow windows in the casements reach out like sunbeams, the curved glass cut perfectly to size; they're like footprints in the snow.

It's the inside that makes me gasp. The hall floor is painted bright blue—as blue as the summer sky. The walls and ceiling are buttercup yellow. Blue rag rugs mark where we are to place our feet, like flagstones in a sunny garden. The hall is completely empty of furniture, just blue floors, yellow walls, and small blue rugs.

Yellow is a happy color, and blue is serene. Isaac smiles

5

at me. I know what he's thinking: We're going to like it here at Pleasant Hill.

The twin spiral staircases in the hall are a wonder. The railings and stairs seem to float upward, like curls of smoke.

An older woman approaches us briskly. "I'm Eldress Mary." She stands in the doorway and gracefully unfolds one arm toward the dining room. "Welcome to Sinai's Holy Plain. Welcome to Heaven on Earth."

Ma smiles. "I'm Mrs. Elizabeth Lipking. These are my three children. I'm hoping you'll take us in."

While Eldress Mary takes us in, I take her in. She must be a New England Shaker: straight-backed and steady-eyed, she's no coy Southern belle. She's dressed head to foot in white. A large white kerchief is tied around her shoulders. Her hair is completely covered by a white bonnet. Her gesturing arm is so elegant, like a dancer's.

She speaks with crisp authority. "You and your children must be famished, Mrs. Lipking. Please sit down in the Elders' Dining Room. The sisters will bring you an early nooning."

She leads us toward the back of the spacious dining room. On the way we pass entrances to two large rooms crowded with chairs. "Those are the Sisters' and Brethren's Waiting Rooms," Eldress Mary tells us.

"What are they waiting for?" Isaac asks. I twist his ear to hush him.

The dining hall is huge, and painted in buttercup yellow and summer-sky blue. Twenty-eight tables with ten chairs apiece—two hundred eighty people eat here.

Eldress Mary guides us to the right, to a small alcove off the dining hall. We sit down on Shaker chairs at a plain, spotless table of honey-colored pine. I've seen chairs like these in Harrodsburg's dry-goods stores. They're straight ladder-backs with woven tape seats. The blue and yellow tapes are an ever-so-slightly darker blue and yellow than the walls and ceiling.

A butter-yellow daffodil stands at attention in a slim blue vase.

Mr. Godfrey shuffles his feet impatiently.

"You may sit," Eldress Mary says.

After Ma sits down, we all take seats around her. "This room is clean," she says admiringly.

Two Shaker sisters walk in with trays of food and crockery and then leave us. We eat cornbread soaked in cream, warm and chunky applesauce, and sweet pickled fruit. There's a peculiar-tasting herbal tea to drink— slightly sweet, slightly smoky, more bracing than calming. The tea tastes like spring.

The food is good, plenty, plain, and simple. It tastes as clean and airy-bright as the room—like eating a daffodil, I think. We eat our fill. I don't remember the last time I ate my fill.

We eat and eat. Even Mr. Godfrey eats as though starving.

Eldress Mary appears again.

"Your children must be tired, Mrs. Lipking," she says briskly. "They'll join the Children's Order within the Center Family to sleep as angels."

Angels?

In haste, a broad-shouldered young man steps from the left door frame, as though he's been waiting for a sign from Eldress Mary. Above the summer-sky-blue floor, his dark shirt and pants hover like a thundercloud.

"Brother John will take your boy to the boys' side of the Center Family dwelling. He'll bathe, clothe himself as an angel, and sleep in his own bed."

"This is Isaac Carl Lipking," Ma says to Brother John.

Brother John turns his head slightly toward Ma. He doesn't speak to her. "Come with me, Brother Isaac." His voice is soft and low.

"Go with Brother John," Ma says.

Ma holds Isaac and whispers in his ear. He rubs his eyes with the back of a dirty hand. His hand comes away wet, streaked in tears. Brother John leads my brother away.

A woman appears in the right doorway.

"This is Sister Emily," Eldress Mary says. "She'll take your daughter to the girls' side of the Center Family dwelling. There she'll bathe, clothe herself as an angel, and sleep in her own bed."

"The girls' side! I thought I'd stay with Ma," I protest.

"Rosemary Elizabeth, no trouble now," Ma says firmly. "You're almost fifteen. Do exactly what the Shakers want and we'll all be safe here."

Mr. Godfrey leans back in his chair and looks at me. "What did I tell you, girl? It's a monastery, nunnery, and boarding school combined."

Sister Emily pays no mind to Mr. Godfrey. "Thee will see your mother after thee has slept. I promise thee. Thee will see your mother every day."

"What's going to happen to Pa?" I've been waiting for hours to ask that question. Despite all the misery he's caused, my heart is pounding. *Mr. Godfrey, please don't tell Pa you left us here.*

Mr. Godfrey stands and steps away from the table. Bits of cow manure and dried mud fall off his boots and powder into a mottled ring around him. Eldress Mary and Sister Emily stare at the floor in alarm.

"I won't be keeping him on," he announces, as though he's a king delivering a royal decree. "Your mother did all his work and hers as well."

An uneasy silence fills the room. Ma's eyes brim with tears. Mr. Godfrey shuffles his feet in embarrassment. More dirt powders from his boots onto the shiny blue floor.

"The missus and I will miss you, Mrs. Lipking."

"He wasn't always like this," Ma whispers.

"I believe you," Mr. Godfrey replies. "You wouldn't have married him otherwise. Moonshine and bourbon are terrible things for a man without the head or the will for them."

Ma and I exchange glances. We are used to keeping the real Pa a secret.

Mr. Godfrey continues. "Carl Lipking can join the army. Both the Union and the Confederates are looking for men who can shoot; either one will gladly take him. He's a deadeye—I'll give him that. He wouldn't be a Kentuckian if he couldn't shoot."

He sweeps his hat toward Eldress Mary and Sister Emily. "Ladies."

This is the signal for the ladies to fuss over a departing man. They'll ask to be remembered and try to press onto him a sweet, or a letter, or a ribbon, or some token of their esteem and affection. The man will bow and kiss the backs of the ladies' hands and declare how pleasant their hospitality was and how fondly it'll be remembered. I've witnessed such pleasantries whenever there have been guests at the Godfreys' home. We'll be fine; this still is Kentucky, after all.

Even so, Eldress Mary and Sister Emily flee silently out the right doorway of the dining room.

Mr. Godfrey eases his thumbs behind his suspenders and laughs as loudly as a braying mule, certainly loudly enough for the Shaker women to hear.

Ma does fuss over him. She tells him that she can't thank him enough and what a pleasure it's been serving him and Mrs. Godfrey. Mr. Godfrey bows, kisses her hand, and says he wishes he could do more for us. Ma assures him that he's done more than enough. She asks to be remembered to Mrs. Godfrey.

"You and your delightful children will be missed, Mrs. Lipking."

Ma blushes and says, "Oh, hush now."

"I won't breathe a word as to your whereabouts." Sunshine glides through the clean windows and catches Mr. Godfrey in a splash of light. I notice how old he is: grizzled hair and beard, stooped shoulders, wrinkled face, missing teeth, trembling hands. With a bow, he stomps out of the blue-and-yellow dining room, leaving a trail of dried muck behind him.

The instant he leaves, Sister Emily rushes back, broom and dustpan in hand. She sweeps up Mr. Godfrey's boot leavings quickly and thoroughly. "As Mother Lee has said, 'There is no dirt in Heaven,'" she remarks, and smiles at me kindly.

"When will I see Ma again?"

"Thee will be reunited with your mother at the evening meal," Sister Emily says. She turns to me. "I'll take thee to the Center Family dwelling now."

Ma gives me an abrupt hug. "Mind the sisters. Be good, you hear?"

"The Center Family lives in the center of Pleasant Hill," Sister Emily announces as she leads me across the lane to a four-storied brick building. Plain but well-made shops and sheds are all around us. Each building has two sets of porches, two sets of doors, two sets of stairs, two sets of outdoor benches, and two flower gardens.

"Why do you have two of everything?"

Sister Emily smiles at me. "As Mother Ann Lee has said, 'The only hope of salvation is separation of the sexes.' We're to seek perfection if we're to live as Heaven on Earth."

"Separation of the sexes? But weren't Adam and Eve *before* the Fall perfection on Earth?" I ask. "'Sleep on, blest pair.' That's from Milton's *Paradise Lost*."

Sister Emily looks startled. She shakes her head. "Thee has been reading the books of the world's people."

"Do you mean," I say slowly, "men and women, boys and girls, don't even talk to each other? Use the same doorway? That's what Shaker separation means?"

"Yea." Sister Emily points to the right. "There are five families at Pleasant Hill. On the east side is the East Family. Our livestock belong to the East Family." She points left. "On the west side is the West Family. The West Family owns the corn and other crops. To the west of the West Family is the West Lot Family. They own the mill."

My head is spinning. *I can't talk to Isaac? Isaac can't talk to Ma?*

She points northeast. "The North Family is down the hill toward the river. They own the quarry. The children live with the Center Family, right here in the center of Pleasant Hill."

My next question just pops out. "Where . . . where did that daffodil come from, the one in the dining room? It's too early for daffodils."

Sister Emily smiles and points to the right. "The East Family has a greenhouse—a building made of glass. It stays warm all winter, so we may grow flowers for special occasions. Mother Ann Lee dearly loved flowers. 'Consider the lilies of the field.' God takes care of all of us."

"Our arrival was a special occasion? That daffodil was for us?"

"Of course! Welcome to Pleasant Hill. Welcome to Heaven on Earth."

The Center Family dwelling is really more like a barn: huge, tall, with a sloping roof. We go through the right-hand door and take the right staircase to the second floor. There are two rooms, each with three beds. Sister Emily smiles again. "This is the girls' side, and your retiring room to share with two other girls in the Children's Order."

Again the walls are buttercup yellow, but here the floors are not painted. They're made of white pine, just like the dining table where we ate. The honey scent of beeswax rises from the floors. There is not a spot of dirt anywhere. Even the windows are as clean as air.

"Everything's so clean," I say. "How pleasant it must be, to live amid such cleanliness." Our dirt-floor cabin wasn't tidy—it was dark and smoky—but Ma did her best.

Sister Emily beams. "As Mother Ann Lee has said—"

" 'There is no dirt in Heaven,' " I chime in.

Sister Emily gives me a peculiar look—half proud that I remembered, half annoyed that she didn't get to repeat it herself.

I smile at her, hoping to make amends. "That's a good saying. I'll have to remember it."

"This is Sister Agnetha. She is responsible for the school sisters."

A large, broad-shouldered woman fills the doorway. Unlike Sister Emily and Eldress Mary, she needs two kerchiefs to reach across her wide shoulders and thick upper arms.

Sister Agnetha smiles, but her tiny black eyes don't shine friendly.

"This is your bed," she says in a deep voice.

Sister Emily has vanished. *Where did she go? Shakers appear and disappear so quickly.*

In front of each bed is a rug. Beside each bed is a nightstand, and at the foot of each bed is a chair. All along the walls, within easy reach, are strips of wood with pegs drilled in every twelve inches or so. On some pegs hang chairs and brooms; others hold white dresses, caps, sunbonnets, aprons, and stockings, each more snowy white than the last.

"You're to clothe yourself as an angel to sleep as one. But first"—here Sister Agnetha points to a dry sink and water pitcher—"wash your hands, face, and neck."

The Shaker soap smells like daffodils. It feels good to be clean after the dust from the road. The linen towel is embroidered with peach-colored roses and smells like lavender and lemons.

Sister Agnetha hands me a long nightgown, perfectly clean and perfectly white. Rather stiffly, she turns her back. I undress quickly and put it on.

"Kneel by your bed and give thanks for all you've been given. Only then may you sleep. Believers sleep flat on their backs with their hands crossed in front, like an angel at rest. Someone will wake you in a few hours."

The little white rug by my bed has an angel crocheted upon it. My knees settle into cuplike depressions on the angel's wings. Others have prayed on this rug. How many sets of knees? And for how many hours?

I kneel and turn my face up to Sister Agnetha. "My brother is only eight years old. Ma and I have to talk to him."

"You're winter Shakers," she says gruffly. "You may talk to him as you wish, as long as it doesn't interfere with your work."

"What's a winter Shaker?" I say to Sister Agnetha's back as she leaves.

The bedclothes, pillowcases, and blankets are snow white and smell of lavender and lemons, just like the towel. And clean, so clean. I sink into them with pleasure.

I wonder where Ma and Baby Anne are sleeping. Does Isaac feel safe? A tiny nudge of alarm pokes my stomach.

Then I roll into a snug ball between warm clouds of lavender-and-lemon-scented bedclothes. My last thoughts are of the daffodil. How did it get to the table so quickly? How did someone know we would be eating there? And how did the food arrive so quickly? The butter-yellow daffodil was so welcoming, so inviting with its promise of spring.

Maybe Pleasant Hill really is Heaven on Earth.

2

I Leap! I Fly!

I sleep soundly until someone shakes my shoulder.

Three young women, all dressed as Shakers, stand over me.

"Yea, you must rise," one says, "before the evening supper bell rings."

I rise. At the bedfoot, ironed and folded neatly, are clothes like theirs: white dress and underclothes, white apron, white cap, and white shoulder kerchief. I'm to wear my own stockings and shoes, I reckon.

Just as Sister Agnetha did, the Shaker girls turn their backs. I dress quickly. We each have our own basin, soap, and towel. We wash our hands. I follow the girls downstairs and to the dining hall.

"This is the Sisters' Waiting Room," the oldest girl says. "'Waiting' means praying: Just as Royal David did, we 'wait upon the Lord.'"

We sit in a huge front room filled with chairs and

crowded with girls and women, all in white. We sit in silence for fifteen minutes, I reckon. Have I ever been with this many people, and all of them female, before?

I count the women and girls in the room: one hundred sixty-four, one hundred sixty-five. . . . There are five girls who look to be about my age. . . . One hundred seventy . . .

The inviting *chink* of plates and cutlery being set on tables in the next room makes my mouth water, but after all that herbal tea in the Elders' Dining Room, my bladder feels set to bursting. In our haste to get here, I didn't look for a chamber pot under my bed. I squirm.

Sister Agnetha stands. So does everyone else.

Then Sister Agnetha turns and glares at me. "What is your name?"

"Rosemary Elizabeth Lipking, ma'am," I stammer.

"A world's name to be sure. It'll be Sister Bess from now on." Sister Agnetha turns, hands on hips, to the smallest of the girls.

"Ma'am? My name is—"

"Didn't you show Sister Bess to the outhouse?"

The smallest girl looks stricken. "I didn't think of it," she whispers.

"Make haste. It's not too late before evening's supper."

The smallest girl takes me down the women's steps, across the lane, and behind the Center Family dwelling to a row of outhouses on the right side of the yard. Whitewashed with blue trim, even the outhouses are spotlessly clean.

"Are there no chamber pots inside the dwellings?" I ask.

"Mother Ann Lee has said, 'Our home is Heaven on Earth. There is no imperfection in Heaven.'"

I groan. "What about in winter?"

"Our supper bell will ring soon," the smallest girl says. "You should make haste, Sister Bess." She gives me a hopeful look and opens an outhouse door.

I go inside and shut the door. "My name is Rosemary Elizabeth Lipking," I mutter, sitting down. "Not Sister Bess."

"Sister Bess, you'll have to go upstairs and wash your hands again," the smallest girl calls to me. "Unclean hands are an imperfection. Make haste."

"My name is Rosemary Elizabeth Lipking, and I'm going as fast as I can!"

After a short pause, the smallest girl says, "Press on your lower stomach. You'll go faster."

"Is that what Mother Ann Lee says?" I ask her through the small half-moon cut out of the door. "What's your name?"

"No, it's what *I* say." She giggles. "We take new names once we're on the Shaker path. I'm Sister Patience."

Up the right staircase to wash my hands; down the right staircase to the door. "Sister Bess, I used to be Ellen Hall," the smallest girl whispers. We cross the lane to the Trustee's Office. "I'll kneel before my square—my place at the table. Do exactly the same things I do."

We rush into the dining room just in time. The girls' table is by the women's door, so we don't disturb anyone.

Even so, Sister Agnetha glares.

Two hundred eighty people kneel by their chairs,

hands folded in silent prayer. No one shuffles feet, or coughs, or sniffs. The women's side is rows of white dresses, white caps, and white kerchiefs. The men's side is rows of dark blue coats and shirts, black pants, and black waistcoats. There are quite a few more women than men. The room is absolutely silent.

A man stands. This must be our signal to do the same, for soon everyone is rising up and sitting at their squares.

Shaker women stagger out of the kitchen carrying white trays heavy with food: cured Kentucky ham, eggs fried in perfect circles, molasses brown bread, sweet pickled fruit, applesauce, milk, and lemonade.

Sister Agnetha picks up her napkin. I look to Ellen Hall for guidance. No one says a word; everyone places a white napkin in her lap. The girls pass the serving bowls to the right. We eat off plain white plates.

I make an open-faced sandwich of ham and eggs on brown bread, the way I do at home.

No one talks while eating—not one word. Sister Agnetha looks at me, her mouth crimped shut. I can tell she's bursting to say something, but she doesn't. I look at her as I eat. *What's wrong?*

The warm applesauce is delicious. It's chunky, not smooth, with syrup the color of dark honey. It's like eating the inside of an apple pie.

The pickled fruit is sweetened crab apples with just enough vinegar for bite.

The girls eat everything on their plates: every crumb, every sliver of ham, every drop of egg, and every scalloped apple. I do the same.

Ma's cooking tastes like smoke because she cooks everything over the hearth fire. Shaker food tastes clean. The simple, distinct flavors of eggs, ham, lemons, apples, and bread and butter shine through.

The girls place their knives, forks, and spoons on the edge of their plates. Even with dirty dishes, our table looks pretty, because each square is exactly the same.

Another bell. Everybody kneels again for another prayer, an after-supper prayer this time. I take this chance to look for Ma and Isaac.

In the far left corner is the boys' table. There's Isaac—we have the same soft reddish-brown curls. He's craning his neck toward the girls' table. We see each other at about the same time. I smile at him and he smiles back.

Now . . . where's Ma?

Sister Agnetha is glaring at me again. I bow my head.

I really pray this time: *Lord, thank you for bringing my family here. I scarcely remember when I didn't feel anxious and as jumpy as a grasshopper in a chicken yard. Please make Pleasant Hill a refuge from Pa, and a safe harbor from the war. I'll work hard so we can all stay here, safe and sound.*

Another bell. We shuffle off to the Sisters' Waiting Room once more and sit quietly for another thirty minutes or so. Then Sister Agnetha stands, and we girls follow her back to our side of the Center Family dwelling. The girls chatter loudly as they clomp up the right staircase.

Sister Agnetha grasps my arm. "Sister Bess," she snaps crossly.

How have I displeased her? I give her my sweetest

Southern belle smile. "I'm sure I've done everything wrong."

She doesn't smile back. Instead she recites:

"Though Heaven has blest us with plenty of food,
Bread, butter, and honey, and all that is good,
We loathe to see mixtures where gentlefolk dine,
Which scarcely look fit for the poultry or swine."

Sister Agnetha looks at me expectantly.

What is she talking about?

"Believers don't mix food together, Sister Bess. Sandwich eating is an imperfection. Also, you must Shaker your plate. That means eat everything upon it, then place your knife, fork, and spoon on the inside edge, facing your chair."

"I ate everything, ma'am." The girls have stopped talking. They're no longer climbing the stairs. They've turned to stare, and my face burns bright red. My voice is shaking. "I Shakered my plate."

Sister Agnetha squares her shoulders. "Nay. You put the blade of your knife to the *outside* edge of your plate. The blade should face the *inside*, as a show of affirmation, peace, and perfection among Believers. As Mother Ann Lee has said, 'Have a place for everything and keep everything in its place.' We are living in Heaven on Earth, Sister Bess. Everything in Pleasant Hill is kept in perfect, heavenly order."

"I'm sorry, ma'am," I say softly. "I'll learn."

"Come with me up the right staircase. There's time."

"Time for what?" I stammer. *What have I done now?*

Sister Agnetha leads me to the retiring room. She points to a row of pegs above my bed. "These are your pegs: pegs thirty-five through thirty-eight. You left your nightgown on your bed. It belongs on peg thirty-five when not in use."

"Yes, ma'am." I hang my nightgown on peg thirty-five. How did she know I left my nightgown on my bed? "I'm sorry. I won't do it again."

"You must take good care of your clothes so they last a long time." Her tone softens a little. "Do you know of Holy Hill, the Believers' village in Canterbury, New Hampshire?"

"No, ma'am."

"At Holy Hill there are eight millponds, paddlewheels, dams, and spillways. Together they control the water that serves seven hundred and fifty people. As we Believers say, when the Canterbury Believers are finished with the water, it is all worn out. Do you perceive the borrowing?"

"Yes, ma'am. I'm to wear these clothes until they're all worn out."

Sister Agnetha nods. "Waste is imperfection. Imperfection is Earth. Perfection is Heaven. Sinai's Holy Plain is Heaven on Earth. . . . We have enough time for the outhouse line before the evening common prayer in the Sisters' Waiting Room."

The Sisters' Waiting Room *again?*

This time we sit erect, with our palms facing up. We sit without moving for at least thirty minutes. Another bell. Sister Agnetha stands up.

As the girls clatter down the women's steps, Sister

Agnetha says, "Sister Bess, you don't have to go to quick worship. You're not a Believer. You may retire to bed, if you choose."

At the Balm of Gilead Church of a Sunday, we sit motionless for hours as Pastor Isthby rails about the sundry imps and demons waiting for us in Hades. But I've heard tell about the goings-on at Shaker quick worship. I've heard tales of the shaking, of the quaking, of the rolling on the floor, of the whirling in circles, of the shrieking, of the stomping of feet, and of the clapping of hands as they dance. Retire to bed? I wouldn't miss a Shaker quick worship even if the circus were in town.

"Oh, no, ma'am," I say politely. "I want to go to quick worship."

Sister Agnetha looks pleased.

"You don't have to worship, unless Mother Ann Lee impels you."

The Meetinghouse is in the middle of Pleasant Hill. It's another plain white building. The women and girls go in the right door. The men and boys go in the left door. We sit on opposite sides of the Meetinghouse.

There are many more people here than there were in the dining room. We sit. And sit. It's just like the Sisters' Waiting Room. *Are the stories about the Shakers not true after all? Do they do nothing but sit—just like the rest of us?*

The same man who stood up before supper now stands up before us. I can tell this is unusual, for everyone looks alarmed; some commence to murmur.

Sister Patience whispers in my ear, "That's Elder Benjamin. He's come all the way from Massachusetts to lead us here at Pleasant Hill."

Elder Benjamin raises his hands. "It's all right. It's all right. Sinai's Holy Plain has received a letter from Holy Mount, from the North Family in New Lebanon, New York. Brothers Samuel, Giles, and Aaron are drafting a letter to President Lincoln, to petition a war exemption for the Believers. Here is the proposed closing."

He holds up a piece of paper, puts on a pair of spectacles, and reads: "'That an order be issued by the proper department, exempting from draft, for army purposes, all societies whose religious principles, and conscientious scruples, of those members prohibits them from the practice of war and bloodshed.'"

Elder Benjamin turns to the men's side of the Meetinghouse. The men turn toward him, their faces anxious and attentive. "Let us pray that our brethren will not be forced into the Army of the Potomac. If our petition is accepted, no Believers will have to fight in this war.

"The brothers will also mention that no veteran Believer accepts a soldier's pension from the 1812 war with England, or the 1846 war with Mexico. To show their gratitude, they intend to invite President Lincoln to Holy Mount and present him with a Believer chair and a barrel of lemonade syrup. That is all."

He sits down.

I'm stunned. The Shakers keep themselves separate in all things, so how do they know about the war?

Suddenly, a big man stands up. "I leap! I fly!" he shouts. He jumps so high I can see daylight between his boots and

24

the floor. The floorboards shudder as he lands; it feels like an earthquake.

Two women stand up and begin to twirl, faster and faster. As they twirl, they sing:

"Love is little, love is low,
Love will make your spirit grow.
Love is little, love is low,
Love will make your spirit grow."

"I leap! I fly!" More young men leap up. More women twirl. The girls stand up and begin to march around the room, stomping their feet and clapping their hands. They march next to me, shouting above their clapping and stomping: "Harvard, Hancock, Tyringham, Shirley, Canterbury, Alfred, Enfield, too. New Lebanon, New Gloucester, Niskayuna . . ."

The rest is a jumble of noise amid the Shaker hubbub.

Across the Meetinghouse, on the men's side, I see Isaac sitting all by himself. He's chewing on his bottom lip. I know that means he's trying hard not to cry. His right hand strokes his left. I know he's pretending to stroke our cat, Lucy.

I still don't see Ma. Maybe she's with Baby Anne. Surely the Shakers don't expect a mother and baby to attend quick worship, not with all this ruckus. Maybe she and Baby Anne have retired for the night?

Isaac and I will see Ma and our baby sister tomorrow.

I wait for the girls to come back around to the girls' chairs. I'm not going to sit alone like Isaac! I jump up and join them. "Harvard, Hancock, Tyringham, Shirley, Canterbury, Alfred, Enfield, too. New Lebanon, New Gloucester, Niskayuna, North Union, South Union, Pleasant Hill, Whittaker, Watervliet, too. . . ."

I've heard of Canterbury. That's where the Shakers wear out the water. Sister Agnetha said that's Holy Hill. I know New Lebanon, too. That's where the brethren live who will petition President Lincoln. That's Holy Mount. The Shakers have Bible names for their villages. Pleasant Hill is Sinai's Holy Plain. North Union is near Cleveland, Ohio. South Union is south of here, near the Mammoth Cave.

I must ask the girls about the others.

Now Isaac has joined a line of boys. Someone has given him a drum and drumsticks. With the first smile I've seen on his face in many a day, he is drumming loudly. The boys march and sing in loud voices.

We girls pass a group of men singing like Christmas carolers:

> "O the simple gifts of God,
>   they're flowing like the ocean,
> And I will strive with all my might
>   to gather in my portion.
> I love, I love the gifts of God.
>   I will be a partaker,
> And I will labor day and night
>   to be an honest Shaker."

Shakers are marching, chanting, twirling, singing, and clapping. The younger men are still leaping and landing hard. Others are whirling. A woman next to me is shrieking:

"More love, more love, Mother Love,
The Heavens are blessing, the angels are calling,
Hosannah, O Zion, more love,
More love, more love, Mother Love . . ."

All this and much more and all at once; the din is as though painted thickly on the air. As they twirl, the Shakers drip sweat. As they stomp, the floorboards quake. As they shriek, the windows fog. As they dance, the kerosene lamps on the ceiling hooks sway and slosh.

This is what a battlefield must be like: the noise, the confusion, the heat, the crush of flying bodies. The only thing missing is the gunfire.

I retreat to a corner.

The Shakers wail and shriek louder, louder, then quickly go quiet. How do they know when to stop? It's dark as Sister Agnetha shoos us out the women's door to the Center Family dwelling.

The girls run up the right staircase, shed clothes, sponge-bathe, slip into nightgowns, pray on their angel rugs, and fall fast, fast asleep.

I stay awake because I have so many questions. Does nobody talk here?

I tell myself I can be perfect in the ways of the Shakers . . . for now. I can be Sister Bess . . . for now. I'll tell Isaac tomorrow, "Do everything they want so we can stay here at Pleasant Hill." Tomorrow I'll find Ma and Baby Anne.

We have to stay together as a family in our new home.

As a treat, we are allowed to sit in Mrs. Godfrey's second-best parlor while Mr. Godfrey reads the war news of an evening. I listen carefully while Isaac gobbles butter cookies until Ma folds his hands in his lap.

Mr. Godfrey told us that Mr. and Mrs. Lincoln were both born in Kentucky. The president is from an abolitionist family; Mary Todd Lincoln is from one of the largest slave-holding families in the Bluegrass. "That explains Kentucky to a tee," he's fond of saying.

I wonder how much of this war the Shakers know about, behind these trim white fences.

The soothing scents of lavender and lemons surround me. I fall asleep, dreaming of Cassandra's scones. The Godfreys' house slave makes the best scones, studded with raisins and dried blueberries, light as a feather.

Ma and I churn the Godfreys' butter and it always tastes delicate and sweet. We have walked the cow pastures for hours, with a sharp eye out for wild garlic. If even one milk cow eats even one bulb, an entire batch of butter will be ruined.

In my dream, Cassandra holds a pretty tray of buttered scones in front of me. A cup of tea is at my elbow.

I know I'm dreaming, for she's smiling at me. "Tomorrow will be much better," she says.

3

Perfections

*G*ong, gong, gong, gong . . . gong.

The loudest bell in the world rings once, twice, thrice . . .

The oldest girl is Sister Jane. She says, "That's the four-thirty bell, Sister Bess. Time to wake and greet the day."

I groan and turn over. Sister Jane grabs me by the arms and pulls me out of bed. I slide onto the cold floor. "We have thirty minutes before morning broad grace in the Sisters' Waiting Room. Make haste."

The other girls are already dressed. They strip their beds and fold all the linens neatly on chairs at their bed-foots. They look so cheerfully busy, I feel ashamed lying on the floor.

This time I'm careful to hang my nightgown on peg thirty-five. I dress in yesterday's clothes.

My stockings are dirty and smell of Mr. Godfrey's

cowsheds. "What about my stockings?" I ask Sister Jane. I hold them up.

Sister Jane reels back in horror at the crusty brown toes and heels.

"Nay," she gasps. "Yesterday's clothes are to be left at your bedfoot, Sister Bess. They'll be clean, dry, and folded by supper. Wear these."

She opens a drawer and gives me a new set of clothes: white underclothes, white gown, white apron, white kerchief to tie around my shoulders, white cap, and white stockings.

I hadn't noticed their feet. All the girls wear plain, black boots—sturdy and for all weathers.

I pull yesterday's clothes off over my head. I poke my head through today's chemise.

"Nay," Sister Jane says again. "You must dress the right side of your body first. Like this." I watch her pretend to dress herself—right arm first through the right sleeve, right leg first into the skirt, right stocking, then right boot. Then, left arm through the left sleeve, left leg through the skirt, left stocking, then left boot.

"Believers sit on the right hand of God," she explains cheerfully. "This is our way of remembering." Sister Jane reaches under my bed. "These are your Believer shoes."

I give Sister Jane a big smile in return. "I can learn the Shaker way of dressing. I'm sure it doesn't take any more trouble, with enough practice."

As I don my clothes right side first, the other girls gather brooms and pans. They sweep and sing:

"Sweep, sweep and cleanse the floor,
Mother's waiting by the door."

They sing the same words again and again.

"That's Mother Ann Lee?" I ask Sister Jane. "Maybe she can tell me where Ma is."

Sister Jane smiles again. "Yes, Mother Ann Lee. Sister Agnetha has told me that I'm to be your explainer. There's a lot to explain."

I step into my Believer shoes in wonder: They fit perfectly. We clatter down the steps and stand in line at the women's outhouses behind the Center Family dwelling. There's a wall of painted white planks running down the middle of the yard to separate the women's lines from the men's lines.

The wind blows brisk and cold. Late-winter snow covers the lawns and trees in sodden heaps. The drifts are gray in the foredawn.

"Why do we have to eat breakfast so early?" I groan.

"We eat in shifts," Sister Jane replies. "There are five hundred people at Pleasant Hill, and we can't all eat together. The children always eat in the first shift."

She fixes her bright smile on me. "Mother Ann Lee died on September eighth, 1784. She's our spiritual mother and founder. She was born in Manchester, England, on Leap Year Day, February twenty-ninth, 1736." Sister Jane claps her hands. "Today is Mother Ann Lee's birthday!

"Mother Ann Lee was imprisoned constantly for her beliefs. When she was released from the filthiest prison in

Britain for the fifth time, she revealed herself to be the Second Coming of our Lord."

"Jesus came back as a woman?" I interrupt in amazement.

Sister Jane keeps talking. "Mother Ann Lee also revealed that God had given her a mission: She was to usher in the new millennium, in the year 2001. It's not that far off, Sister Bess. Mother Ann Lee came to America and started the first Believer village in Niskayuna, in New York, near Albany. That was in 1780. Its spiritual name is Wisdom's Valley.

"In 1805, three Believers from New Lebanon, New York, walked all the way to the Kentucky River to start Pleasant Hill. More than one thousand miles through forests, over mountains, fording rivers, fleeing from wild beasts—"

"Wait, wait," I interrupt again. I can't get past my big question. "Jesus came back as a woman?"

Sister Jane says evenly, "It's what Believers believe."

"You believe it?"

"Yes," she says, as though daring me to contradict her. But before I can, she goes on. "You may not ask questions in the Sisters' Waiting Room, or during grace in the dining room, or in the Meetinghouse. Those times belong to God in sweet Union."

"So when may I ask questions, then?"

"When we work, Sister Bess. As Mother Ann Lee has said, 'Hands to work, hearts to God.'"

After the outhouse, we race upstairs to wash our hands with the soap that smells of daffodils and to dry them on the towels that smell of lavender and lemons. Then to the Sisters' Waiting Room to sit in chairs and pray. Palms up; no talking. Some of the girls are dozing. I rest my eyelids, too.

In the dining room, kneel and pray; another silent meal of delicious, simple Shaker food. We kneel and pray again after we break our fast. We rise and go out the women's steps. It's still dark outside.

"Attend, Sister Bess," Sister Agnetha commands. "What would you like to do as an affirmation of Pleasant Hill?"

I blurt out, "I like to read."

Instantly, I know this is a mistake, for Sister Agnetha squares her shoulders. "Nay. As Mother Ann Lee has said, 'Hands to work, hearts to God.' There must be something you'll do."

What would she like to hear? What would I like to do? "I'd like to learn how to make Shaker applesauce. It's delicious."

Sister Agnetha looks at me, genuinely happy. "Wonderful! To the kitchen."

I smile up at her and glow.

Sister Emily guides me toward a mountain of apples. "Thee will peel."

I remember that I can ask questions when I'm working, but Sister Jane is not here. Who will my explainer be?

I put down the apple and paring knife and look for Sister Emily. She's standing on a short ladder in front of a stove, stirring something in an enormous kettle the size of a pickle barrel. "Um . . . Sister Emily?"

She looks down at me in surprise. "Why aren't thee peeling apples?"

"Sister Agnetha asked Sister Jane to be my explainer. She's not here."

"Nay. There will be plenty of time for that. The apples!"

"But—"

"How many hands did God give thee?" Sister Emily demands. "And how many mouths?"

I know what that means: Hands to work. I go back to my mountain of apples.

Every once in a while, a sister comes by to gather peeled apples. She appears just when the first in my pile is beginning to turn brown. How does she know that?

I'm guessing it's about eleven o'clock, and my hands and forearms are slippery with apple juice. Two sisters come into the kitchen carrying two twigs apiece, each about as wide as my thumb and as long as my forearm. Immediately, the peeling, chopping, stirring, and cooking stop. Everyone is absolutely silent.

The two sisters carefully peel the bark from the twigs. The wood is *wick*, still green: these twigs are alive. The sisters roll the twigs on a chopping board until they shine with sap. Then they beat bowls of cake batter with the twigs.

Everyone else stands, head bowed in silent prayer.

After getting a good look, I bow my head too.

What on Earth?

After the cakes are in the ovens, everyone returns to work.

The noon dinner bell rings. My pile of apples is gone.

I run back to the girls' side of the Center Family dwelling to wash my hands—the daffodil soap and lemon-and-lavender-scented towel again. Broad grace in the Sisters' Waiting Room; kneeling and praying by my square.

We sit silently and eat steaming applesauce, cornbread soaked in cream, slices of beef, carrots, and potatoes. We drink lemonade.

This time I pay particular attention to the applesauce. I peeled each and every one of these apples. This morning, I peeled enough apples to feed five hundred people! Someone else sliced them perfectly into eighths, each the shape of a new moon.

Sister Emily boiled the apple syrup, in that kettle as big as a pickle barrel. Shaker applesauce tastes so good. The sauce is hot, but the apples are still as crunchy as fruit right off the tree. How do they manage that? Maybe I'll learn what's in the apple syrup. Maybe I'll find out about the twigs as well.

But first I have to find my family. After another broad grace in the Sisters' Waiting Room, I approach Sister Agnetha.

"I need to talk to my brother, ma'am," I say firmly. "You promised me, yesterday afternoon. I worked hard all morning. His name is Isaac Carl Lipking and he's only eight years old."

"You may speak to your brother. Brother John will accompany him to the front yard of the Trustee's Office in a few minutes."

"Yes, ma'am. Thank you."

"Then you will go to the girls' school, on the fourth floor of the Center Family dwelling, on the right side. Mind you walk up the right staircase."

"Yes, I know, ma'am. Women and girls bear right in all ways. Men and boys bear left in all ways."

I stand in front of the Trustee's Office and wait. It seems ages ago that the Lipkings walked up these stairs and gazed at the buttercup-yellow walls and spotless blue floors for the first time. Do I dare take a ladder-back chair from the Elders' Dining Room? Should I ask Eldress Mary first? Or another adult? Shaker chairs are so comfortable, and I'm tired from peeling apples.

Brethren trot up the lane with shepherd crooks, following a herd of sheep. The men don't even look in my direction.

I drag a ladder-back chair from the Elders' Dining Room out onto the lawn. I sit and wait for Isaac.

After a few moments I see Brother John leading Isaac from the boys' side. I jump up and Isaac flies into my arms.

As I hug him, I wonder: How did Sister Agnetha tell Brother John I wanted to see my brother, if Shaker men and Shaker women can't talk to each other?

"Isaac! I'm so happy to see you!"

"Rosemary Elizabeth, where's Ma?" he demands. "I haven't seen her, have you? I've looked at supper, and breakfast, and nooning, but I can't find her. Where is she?"

Cold fear clutches my heart. "I haven't seen her, either."

I glance at Brother John, who is looking down the

lane toward the East Family's vegetable garden. Even if he had seen her, he'd never tell me.

"I'll ask Sister Agnetha, or maybe Eldress Mary knows. Maybe . . . there's a girls' side and a boys' side; maybe there's . . . a baby girls' side?" Even I know that's ridiculous. *Has Ma left Pleasant Hill with Baby Anne? That's impossible.*

"Where's Ma?" Isaac wails. His eyes fill with tears.

"Are you well?" I ask quickly. "What tasks have you addressed?"

Isaac sniffs. "I've been milking cows. Just like home."

I hug him again. "I'll talk to you after every nooning, after the broad grace. Meet me here in the front yard of the Trustee's Office tomorrow. I'll find out about Ma. All right?"

"They made me take a sponge bath last night," Isaac complains. "We're to take a bath every night. Something about being clean in Heaven. This isn't Heaven. This is Kentucky!"

Brother John chuckles into his ample beard.

"I have to take a sponge bath every night, too. We all do. Isaac, I'll find out what happened to Ma. I promise. Listen to me." I lean closer and whisper in his ear, "Don't complain to the brethren about anything! The Shakers want us to be perfect. Can you do that?"

Isaac nods, and strokes his right hand with his left.

"Just do everything they want, so we can stay here. Here we'll be fed well, and we'll be safe, away from the war." I whisper, more softly, "Safe from Pa."

Isaac squirms. I can almost see his troubled thoughts cross his face, like thunderclouds across a blue summer sky.

But I have to be sure. "I'll meet you tomorrow after the nooning broad grace, in front of the Trustee's Office."

I turn toward Brother John and say loudly, "Ask Brother John if you're not sure about the time." Then I whisper again, "Promise me you'll try to be perfect. Promise me you won't complain about anything."

Isaac gives me another big hug. "I'll meet you tomorrow," he says. As he walks across the lane to the Center Family dwelling, my brother puts his hand in Brother John's hand.

I run up the four flights of stairs to the girls' schoolroom. Sister Agnetha is standing in front of the class, pointing to a map of an intact United States.

I gasp. Sister Agnetha's our teacher? I didn't expect to see her sour face again until supper!

She squares her shoulders and glares at me, as usual. "Sister Bess, light here." She points to a desk and chair that are perfectly aligned with her desk and chair. "You're to sit next to me until I've learned what you've learned."

"Yes, ma'am."

The schoolroom is small and hot. The five other girls sit behind desks and listen attentively as Sister Agnetha talks about the Shakertown of Union Branch in Gorham, Maine. "It was the Gorham Elder Joseph who wrote the Believer song 'Simple Gifts.' To the world's people, this song explains everything they think they need know about us."

Sister Jane writes something on a slip of paper. Ellen Hall—Sister Patience—gazes dreamy-eyed out the window toward the horse pasture.

After singing all three verses of "Simple Gifts," we're allowed outside for an hour's diversion.

Behind the Center Family dwelling is the water house. I haven't seen it before. All around the water house are apple, plum, peach, and quince trees, the branches held up with forked sticks. So that's where the fruit comes from.

We quench our thirst with buckets of well water. Even the Shaker water is clean and pure. It has no taste at all.

On the other side of the orchard is the boys' play yard. I watch the boys stomp down the left staircase and burst out of their door like a buffalo stampede. There are seven boys.

Isaac climbs a horse chestnut tree with a young man. Lambs in the sheepfold watch, woolly chins rising, as they climb up, and up, and up.

At last these Shaker girls act like other girls I know. We jump rope and play hopscotch and jacks. The schoolgirls must have been testing me with their games, for as recess ends, they crowd around with their questions.

"Where do y'all hail from?"

"How did y'all end up at Pleasant Hill?"

"Where are your parents?"

"How long y'all fixing to stay?"

"From near Harrodsburg," I answer. "I grew up on Mr. Godfrey's dairy farm. My mother brought my brother, my baby sister, and me here. I don't know how long we're going to stay."

I won't tell these Shaker girls about Pa. How much

easier it is to say nothing. They'll assume he's in the war.

"I haven't seen Ma. We've been in Pleasant Hill for more than twenty-four hours. The Shakers don't keep mothers apart from their children, do they?"

The girls become still as well water. They exchange uneasy glances.

"Have you tried the women's side of the hospital?" Sister Patience asks. "It's to the west of the West Family's dwelling, near the corncrib."

"If she were sick, somebody would have told me. Isn't that right?"

Why are the girls so quiet all of a sudden? Sister Jane puts her arm around my shoulders. "I'm sorry, Sister Bess," she says softly.

"Why?" I catch my breath.

"Parents leave their children at Pleasant Hill," Sister Jane continues. "When my pa joined the army, Ma left and went home to Wisconsin. She said traveling with me would be too slow and too dangerous. I'm to earn my keep here until this cruel, cruel war is over. She said she'd come back and fetch me; she promised. She'll walk right through the front gates and fetch me."

I stare at Sister Jane. Her blue eyes gaze back at me, full of kindness.

"Ma died." Sister Patience speaks up softly. "Pa rides with Morgan."

"All of us," Sister Jane says. "We're either orphans or our parents left us at Pleasant Hill. Only one, Sister Amy, has her father here, in the East Family dwelling. He talks to her after breakfast."

Sister Amy's black eyes shine. "I talk to Pa every day."

Tiny Sister Sarah starts to cry. Sister Jane puts her other arm around her.

"The story is," Sister Jane continues, "Sister Agnetha was left here when her ma ran off with a gambling man from New Orleans. She's been here thirty years since."

"Isaac, Baby Anne, and I are not orphans!"

"Of course you're not," another girl says. She pats my hand. "I'm Sister Lucy."

"We have a cat named Lucy." With the heel of my hand, I push tears away from my eyes. "She's as sleek as a seal and has kittens, five of them, with fuzzy black fur and white boots. I could bear it," I say, my voice breaking, "if Lucy and her kittens were here. I used to whisper secrets to her while she nursed her kittens."

The girls again exchange uneasy glances.

Now what?

Sister Lucy sighs sadly. "As Mother Ann Lee has said, 'In Heaven there are no extraneous animals. Extraneous animals are not in keeping with perfect, Heavenly order.'"

"Extra . . . what? *What* kind of animals?"

"Cats or dogs," Sister Patience explains. "And pet birds. They're an imperfection. There are no pets in Heaven, so there are no pets here in Heaven on Earth."

"That's not true!" I shout. Yet it *is* true, I realize in horror: In this Heaven I have seen no sheepdogs, no barn cats, and no pampered parakeets in fancy cages. I haven't seen a single pet since Mr. Godfrey left us here. It seems as if it's been weeks already, and it's only been since yesterday morning.

Sister Jane adds, "Mother Ann Lee also said, 'Speech is a human affirmation, a gift by the grace of God.' Among the Shakers, talking to animals is an imperfection. Even if Lucy were here, you wouldn't be allowed to speak to her." She pauses thoughtfully. "Parents come back."

I can't tell if Sister Jane is talking to me or to herself.

Her gaze lifts up, toward the front gate. "They do come back, all the way from Wisconsin."

No one says anything as Sister Agnetha rings the school bell.

"Ma promised we'd stay together."

Again Sister Agnetha shakes the school bell, harder this time.

We climb the stairs on the right side of the Center Family dwelling all the way to the fourth floor, back to the girls' schoolroom.

I can live without Lucy and her kittens, for now, if it means we're safe from Pa. But Lucy's sleek black face rises before me, her bright green eyes hurt and reproachful.

When we're dismissed for the day, I stand in front of Sister Agnetha.

"The girls think Ma has gone," I say. I try hard to keep the quaver out of my voice. "They think she's left us here. That can't be true."

"I'm sorry, Sister Bess," Sister Agnetha says softly. "She went back to the world's people during quick worship last evening. We Believers don't call them girls, by the way; they're school sisters."

"That can't be true," I whisper, "about Ma."

"A first-stage brother took her back to Harrodsburg."

"A stage brother?" I'm bewildered. "A . . . a stage-coach driver?"

"No. No, a first-stage brother—a brother who's not a full Believer yet. He's only at the first stage. Although Believers frown on it, he can converse with women still."

"When is she coming back?" Dread chills me from the inside out. "Is Baby Anne gone too?"

"Only God can determine when your mother will return. The West Family dwelling has a nursery. Your sister is in their care."

All I can do is stare in horror at Sister Agnetha. Isaac and I are almost grown, but how could Ma have left Baby Anne behind?

Ma . . . how could you? There must some mistake. . . .

Sister Agnetha looks outside, and I follow her gaze. Late-winter snow covers the budding apple trees. The snow looks like apple blossoms: purest white, as pure white as the Shaker clothes I'm wearing, come to think of it.

"Use this time, Sister Bess," she says softly. "It's the simple gift. Use this time God has given you on Sinai's Holy Plain."

Sister Jane's story must be true, then. Sister Agnetha's ma left her here thirty years ago; she's feeling sorry for me. She thinks my ma has done the same.

No! It can't be true!

4

Imperfections

Before supper: sitting, palms up, in the Sisters' Waiting Room. A bell rings—thirty minutes later, I reckon. The dining room: kneel and pray again. Supper: applesauce—somebody else must have peeled these apples, since I was in school—ham, potatoes, molasses brown bread, and lemonade. We eat carrots from what must be the biggest root cellar in Kentucky.

This evening's supper sits like ashes in my mouth.

How could Ma leave us? I saw Baby Anne this afternoon, sleeping soundly in the West Family's quiet, spotless nursery. We're no trouble, my sister, my brother, and I. Isaac and I have always worked hard.

For dessert, squares of white cake are brought to the tables.

The cake is plain, as white as our clothes, with no icing. Despite the silence, I can sense the excitement about this cake. As they eat, the Shakers nod at one another and smile.

The twigs. This is the cake those sisters prepared with the twigs this morning. Why on earth did they beat the cake batter with twigs?

My piece is gone in a few bites. It tastes . . . almost like fruit, but sweeter. I'm glad to have something good to think about, if only for a moment.

After supper: kneel and pray again. This time I really do pray: *Heavenly Father, please bring Ma back to us. Isaac and I will work hard to be perfect. She'll be so proud of us, she'll want us back.*

Baby Anne is close to perfect—she's a beautiful baby. When Ma returns, we'll all be right here, safe and perfect, waiting for her.

Please bring Ma back, for Isaac and Baby Anne, if not for me. Isaac pines for her something fierce. Baby Anne must know something is wrong.

Why would Ma leave us here?

The Sisters' Waiting Room again for another broad grace: palms up, thirty minutes until the bell. Sister Agnetha stands as our signal to go to quick worship. If I'm quiet about it, I can tell Isaac about Baby Anne in quick worship.

At the Meetinghouse, Elder Benjamin makes a few announcements, mostly about the war. He addresses all his comments to the left side, the men's side. The sisters listen eagerly, too, of course. Just a week ago Confederate president Jefferson Davis was inaugurated in the pouring rain in front of the Confederate States of America capitol in Richmond, Virginia. There were wild celebratory parties as far away as Bardstown, right here in northern Kentucky.

A few days ago Nashville, Tennessee, fell to the Union forces. The Union now controls the Tennessee River.

"Once the Union controls the southern rivers, especially the part of the Mississippi that's in Rebel hands," Elder Benjamin says softly, "this war is as good as won.

"The president's son, William Wallace Lincoln, died on February twentieth. He was twelve years old." He sits down.

The Shakers groan, then murmur. *Of course the Shakers are Unionists,* I think. *Their first community was started in New York.* It is a surprise, though; I thought religions weren't supposed to take sides.

That is so sad, about Willie Lincoln.

"I leap! I fly!" A group of grinning young men jump out of their seats as one. Their Believer boots make a resounding *thud* as they land.

They begin to sing:

"'Tis the gift to be simple, 'tis the gift to be free,
'Tis the gift to be down where we ought to be.
And when we find ourselves in the place just right,
'Twill be in the valley of love and delight."

I run over to Isaac, who is with the boys, beating the drum again.

I have to speak quickly. "Isaac, Baby Anne is safe! She's in the West Family's nursery. Her dress is beautiful, all lace and embroidered peach-colored rosebuds. Three sisters attend her, and—"

Isaac stops beating the drum. "Where's Ma?"

I take a deep breath to speak, but . . .

Sister Agnetha pulls me away from my brother. "A sister can't go to the brethren's side of the Meetinghouse."

"But that's my brother!" *She was so nice this afternoon!*

Sister Agnetha twirls me around. "A sister can't go to the brethren's side of the Meetinghouse!"

I take another deep breath. *Perfect. Perfect.* "Yes, ma'am."

"Stop calling me ma'am, Sister Bess!" she orders. "I'm Sister Agnetha."

Why is she so angry? "Yes, ma'—Yes, Sister Agnetha." I say her name as meekly as I can, but I doubt she heard me, what with the rising din.

"Go as Mother Lee compels you." Yet it is she who compels me toward the girls, who are stomping, clapping, and chanting: "Hancock, Harvard, Tyringham, Shirley, Canterbury, Alfred . . ."

I join the marching girls, hoping for another chance to talk to Isaac. The girls' chain winds around to the center of the Meetinghouse. There is Isaac, banging on the drum as two boys shout:

"I have a little drum that Mother gave to me,
The prettiest little drum that ever you did see.
I'll drum night and day. Yes, I'll drum night and day,
To call volunteers to fight sin away."

I grab his collar. "Isaac! I'm not supposed to talk to you—"

Black-coated men turn their shoulders against me in

47

horror. The backs of their necks are the same bright scarlet as a redbird's wings.

Sister Agnetha grabs me by the shoulders. "You're on the wrong side again!" she shouts in my ear. "Sister Bess! Never go to the brethren's side of the Meetinghouse. Do I make myself clear?"

"I'm sorry!" I shout back, but it's so loud, every Shaker worshiping separately, that no one hears.

Sister Agnetha pushes me again toward the girls.

I bump into a woman. She's red-faced, twirling and shrieking:

"More love, more love, Mother Love.
The Heavens are blessing, the angels are calling,
'Hosannah, O Zion, more love.'
More love, more love, Mother Love."

I spin around frantically in the bedlam. *Where is Isaac?* I don't hear his drum, but it's so loud in quick worship I can't even hear myself think. The girls wend their way into the center again. A chain of young men are stomping, clapping, and shouting nonsense: "Yo, Niskayuna! Yo, ho, ho! Niskayuna! Niskayuna! Yo, ho, ho!"

I spy Isaac with the drum, running out of the Meetinghouse through the men's door. I can't run across the Meetinghouse to stop him—that would be an imperfection.

Brother John runs after Isaac. Sister Agnetha grabs me by the shoulders once again and pushes me toward the stomping and clapping girls.

I shout, even though he can't possibly hear me, "I'll

explain tomorrow! After the nooning! Tomorrow! I'm not supposed to talk to you now!"

"Sister Jane, why was that cake so well received last night? Do you remember? It was white, and everyone had a piece."

It's foredawn, and we are standing at the women's outhouses. The only time I can ask my explainer questions is when we wait in this line.

Sister Jane beams at me. "I've already told you: Yesterday was Mother Ann Lee's birthday. She was born on Leap Year Day, February twenty-ninth, 1736. She was partial to peaches, but of course there are no fresh peaches this time of year. Instead, Believers flavor her birthday cake with the essence of peaches."

Mother Ann Lee again. I should have known.

"As Mother Lee has said, 'Cut a handful of peach twigs which are filled with sap at this season of the year. Peel the bark, clip the ends, and bruise them, and beat the cake batter with them. The ministrations will impart a delicate peach flavor to the cake.'

"Every Believer in every Believer town celebrated her birthday last night. Mother Ann Lee's cake tasted like peaches, didn't it?"

"I reckon," I say slowly. "I liked it."

Sister Jane smiles. "Believers are certain her cake tastes *exactly* like peaches. We celebrate all our birthdays on Mother Ann Lee's birthday. That means happy birthday, Sister Bess!"

"My birthday is on June eighteenth."

Sister Jane's smile cools, as though I've said something

wrong but she doesn't want to hurt my feelings. "All Believers have the same birthday, on Leap Year Day, February twenty-ninth. Or March first."

Her eyes are now as politely chilly as her smile.

"I reckon my birthday could be on February twenty-ninth. Or March first," I say slowly. *For now.* "Happy birthday, Sister Jane."

"Happy birthday." Sister Jane opens the outhouse door. "You can go first."

While peeling apples later this morning, I wonder if it's fair to make everyone have the same birthday. I like having my birthday in June. Mrs. Godfrey gave me some of her roses for my birthday. Last spring she gave Ma a milk bucket full of lilies-of-the-valley on Isaac's birthday.

Around me kitchen sisters peel, chop, stir, bake, roast, slice, churn, scrub, and sweep. Some of them burst into song as they cook. They cook joyfully for five hundred people, in two shifts—six meals a day.

I won't ask Sister Jane about the Shaker birthday. It makes me feel lonesome, though, to see how contented she is, they are, in their perfect, heavenly order.

"Happy birthday," I say to a kitchen sister who is mashing potatoes in a bowl the size of a wagon wheel. She gives me a radiant smile.

After broad grace in the Sisters' Waiting Room, Sister Agnetha grasps me by the arm.

"Yes, ma'am—I mean, Sister Agnetha?"

Her face is purple with rage. "Yesterday afternoon, you left a Believer chair outside by the Trustee's Office.

Chairs belong inside and not outside. It could have rained or snowed on a perfect Believer chair."

"But I—"

"A perfect Believer chair! 'A place for everything and everything in its place.'" Sister Agnetha gives my arm a rough shake. "As Mother Ann Lee has said, 'in keeping with perfect, heavenly order.'"

"I won't take a chair outside again," I say meekly. "I promise."

Is that why she was so angry with me last night at quick worship? Over a chair? Or over my not being perfect?

"Happy birthday," I call out as Sister Agnetha stomps toward the women's side of the dining room, a trail of school sisters in her wake.

Once again, I firm my resolve. Isaac, Baby Anne, and I *can* be perfect. Safe from the war, safe from Pa, and Ma proud of us. I can be perfect. Would it be so awful for now, in the face of all this kindness, to cast aside Rosemary Elizabeth Lipking?

I walk silently to the women's side of the dining room. I kneel and pray silently. I eat silently. I Shaker my plate perfectly, then look at Sister Agnetha, hoping she'll notice.

She doesn't notice.

This year, after a cold spring, summer comes early to Kentucky. It's mid-May and already hot by the nooning. Yet no one slows down on account of the weather. There are floors to sweep, meals to prepare, animals to feed, cows to milk, gardens to tend, thread to spin, dye, and weave into cloth, clothes to sew, brooms to make, cows to milk, cheese to hang, and butter to churn. Every moment of every day is taken with work, eating, or praying. Hands to work, hearts to God.

After quick worship, the Shakers' clothes are as heavy with sweat as if they'd been left out in the rain. We school sisters run to the water house and drink buckets of cool water before our sponge baths. On a particularly hot evening, I poured a bucket of water over my head. It was deliciously cold on my scalp. Sister Agnetha was shocked; I've not done that since.

I've continued to work in the kitchen. For weeks all I did was peel apples. Since then I've wax-sealed gallons and gallons of Shaker applesauce into firkins and wooden pails. Before the war, Pleasant Hill's applesauce was sold as far away as Savannah, Georgia. Now it's stored in the ice-house for winter and for after the war.

I've learned the secret to Shaker applesauce. Soft McIntosh apples are peeled, then boiled down into rich, thick syrup. Then crunchy Pippin apples are peeled; Sister Barbara slices them into perfect eighths. The Pippin slices are added to the vat of bubbling syrup. The Shakers add no spices. Shaker applesauce tastes more like apples than any other applesauce I've ever eaten.

I have moved on to lemonade. I smell of lemons; even my hair smells of lemons. I don't mind. I smell considerably better than I did on Mr. Godfrey's dairy farm.

Shaker lemonade calls for lemons, sugar, and very cold water. Roll the lemons well, and squeeze out the juice.

Here's the secret: Boil the skins, skim off the oil, and then add the lemon-infused water to the lemonade. Each cup requires three chunks of ice—no more, no less. Shaker lemonade tastes more like lemons than any other lemonade I've tried.

I've put up jars and jars of Shaker lemonade syrup.

Isaac follows Brother John the way a lamb follows its mother. We meet in front of the Trustee's Office each day after the nooning. On sunny days we walk to the front gates of Pleasant Hill. Isaac watches and waits for Ma.

In March and April I caught myself hoping, listening for Mr. Godfrey's squeaky oxcart that would return Ma to us. Now, in May, I've stopped hoping. But Isaac hopes still.

On an afternoon in late May, I'm hot and discouraged. I spy a copy of the *Cincinnati Enquirer* in Pleasant Hill's mailbox. It's only a week old. This is how Elder Benjamin knows so much about the war. The Shakers subscribe to the Cincinnati paper!

I read the headlines quickly and sum them up for Isaac. "Yorktown, Williamsburg, and Norfolk, Virginia, have been evacuated prior to siege." Isaac looks intently down the Harrodsburg Pike. "There's going to be a siege at Vicksburg, Mississippi, too."

Isaac says nothing. He shades his eyes against the sun, all the better to watch for Ma.

It's not my newspaper, and I'm already in enough trouble with Sister Agnetha. I roll it up and put it back in the mailbox.

"It must be the war," I say to Isaac, as I say every sunny afternoon. It's the war that keeps Ma from fetching us. "Sister Jane's mother is in Wisconsin. She got a letter from her the other day. It said, 'Travel is impossible.'"

"Travel is impossible," Isaac echoes. "How far away is Wisconsin?"

"Far north. Sister Jane says there's snow in Rhinelander, Wisconsin, six months of every year."

I don't say what I'm thinking—that Mr. Godfrey's dairy farm is only ten miles down the Harrodsburg Pike.

"Travel is impossible," Isaac repeats, his gaze fixed firmly on the Pike.

Brother John is teaching Isaac how to make chairs and Believer shoes. Soon he'll learn the rest of the brethren's chores: animal care, candle making, beekeeping, plowing, gardening, grain threshing, haymaking, and carpentry and cabinetmaking. He'll learn how to make cheese, butter, and cream.

Isaac might be as fine a dairyman as Mr. Godfrey someday.

Eventually, boys learn all of the men's work and girls learn all of the women's work. If Ma doesn't fetch us, this means I'll learn how to cook every Shaker dish, wash and iron every garment, and make thread, cloth, clothes, and Shaker brooms.

Heavenly Father, please bring Ma to Pleasant Hill.

A miracle: My worn clothes and used bed linens disappear from my bedfoot each morning; each afternoon my clean and freshly ironed clothes appear on my pegs and in my drawer space, and my bed is freshly made.

Now I know how this miracle happens. I dread working in the laundry. All that steaming water, and in this heat!

Another miracle explained: Before dawn, brethren leave sides of beef or pork, plucked chickens, crates of fruit and vegetables, and boxes and boxes of eggs by the kitchen door for the sisters to prepare. The victuals are always waiting for us when we kitchen workers arrive.

Now I know how the food gets to us. But another mystery remains unanswered: Why isn't it taken by varmints? Foxes, opossums, and raccoons have a keen, unrelenting appetite for chickens and eggs. I wonder—for how long is the food left undefended at the kitchen door, between the brethren leaving and the sisters arriving? Whose job is it to keep the varmints at bay?

Elder Benjamin won't allow varmint traps to be set. The Shakers don't kill animals except for food.

Days in late June dawn early. It's already hot. We apple peelers, lemonade makers, and bread bakers hurry up the walkway toward the kitchen door. The sisters are chattering about their dreams. It seems they always dream of angels, each angel dream more fantastic and extraordinary than the last.

On this particular morning, there stand ten brethren, shirtless, setting three wrapped sides of beef and boxes of eggs by the kitchen door.

The sisters gasp. A few of them scream and cover their eyes with their hands. Two swoon and tumble to the ground.

The shocked brethren scatter into the dawn's half-light.

Mother Ann Lee's separation of the sexes! Their error is not only a gross imperfection; it's a deep crack in the perfect, heavenly firmament of Pleasant Hill.

All morning, as I peel apples and squeeze lemons, I think about those half-dressed brethren and the sisters' horrified faces. All of the Shakers were doing what they were supposed to be doing: Hands to work, hearts to God. If the brethren had left a minute or two earlier, the gross imperfection would not have occurred and the sisters would not have screamed and the brethren would not have fled from the kitchen door. The heavenly firmament of Pleasant Hill would not have torn asunder.

All morning, the kitchen sisters are quiet, their pale faces troubled and fearful. All day today, I reckon, there will be heartfelt prayers begging for God's grace, begging to be let into Heaven's perfection on Earth once again.

I reckon the brethren will get up even earlier from now on. Or they'll leave the victuals by the kitchen door after quick worship and take turns guarding it all night, or until they hear the kitchen sisters hurrying up the path.

I reckon the sisters will speak louder about their angel dreams, as a way to warn the brethren of their presence. No matter how hot and sticky it is, the brethren will never go shirtless again.

I've lived here long enough to know: Shaker perfection is a complicated business.

*

Every night now, I dream of Ma. I dream that Sister Emily takes my hand and leads me to the Elders' Dining Room. The same daffodil, in the same blue vase, is waiting for us. Ma is waiting, too, glowing with loving-kindness, her arms outstretched. Isaac comes out of nowhere and rushes into her arms.

Ma looks at me, smiling. *Let's find Baby Anne. Let's go home, Rosemary Elizabeth.*

Home.

I've not said one word to anyone at Pleasant Hill about Pa. Not one word. Not one school sister has asked about him, either. Somehow they know enough not to; their silence fills me with shame, but also with relief.

Every day, after the nooning broad grace, Isaac and I meet in front of the Trustee's Office. Someone has placed an iron bench in the front yard for us so we won't have to sit on the wet grass.

Every day Isaac chatters excitedly about something Brother John is teaching him. I tell him about Baby Anne; I visit her every day after the breakfast broad grace. She has a tooth coming in, and the nursery sisters have made her a teething ring out of a circle of black walnut wood set deep within layers of the softest Shaker cotton.

But Isaac doesn't want to listen to talk about Baby Anne. Now, when I talk about Ma coming for us someday, he has a patient look in his eyes. It's as though he's waiting politely for me to stop talking, so he can again work the subject back to what he and Brother John are doing.

When Isaac does visit the nursery, he stands stiff-legged before Baby Anne's cradle, elbows in, for five minutes at most. He's always got a good reason to leave. That he might be losing interest in the Lipkings scares me more than anything. What will happen to my brother, adrift with no family? Ma would want us united and hopeful for better times.

"Let's go to the front gates. Mr. Godfrey might be bringing Ma to Pleasant Hill today."

"If you want to," Isaac replies. "Brother John and I are making candle boxes from bird's-eye pecan. Did you know candle boxes are supposed to hang from the ceiling, so the mice won't eat the tallow? They'll eat candles made from beeswax, too."

I say softly. "Isaac, don't you want to watch and wait for Ma? We've never missed a sunny afternoon."

Isaac's eyes tear up. "I'm done waiting," he says, in a voice so soft I'm not sure I heard him. He looks toward the Center Family carpenter shop. "There's Brother John." He jumps up and runs.

This is your doing, Ma, I think bitterly. *How does it feel, to know that your nine-year-old son no longer hopes for you?*

I know that Baby Anne, at least, is glad to see me. She gurgles and coos and reaches her chubby arms out to me when I walk through the West Family's nursery door.

The nursery sisters can't stop talking about Baby Anne. She is the smartest, the sweetest, the most peaches-and-cream, the most adorable baby who ever lived. They call her Angelica instead of Anne. She is perfect.

When I hold Baby Anne, the nursery sisters' arms reach out to take her, as though I'm just a visitor. As I walk out the door at the end of my time with her, the three sisters quickly turn their backs and hover around Baby Anne's crib, as though they are protecting my own sister from me.

Ma? Isaac and Baby Anne are slipping away from us. We're safe here, well fed, well clothed, and well shod, but you have to come back. When we first came to Pleasant Hill, I was afraid we wouldn't be perfect enough. We worked so hard to please.

Now Isaac is . . . too perfect. Can that be?

And me? Am I becoming too perfect, too?

5

Oh, Be Joyful

The school sisters and brethren are picking apples—separately, of course—on an endless June afternoon when it seems as though the sun will never get around to setting. Isaac again climbs the horse chestnut tree with the same young man I've seen him with before. He is older than Isaac, older than me.

He tosses his shade hat into the air; it floats to the ground. In bright sunlight his hair is as red as a new penny.

I've seen him carrying milk pails from the dairy to the cheese sheds. He looks like a triangle, with broad shoulders and a narrow waist. Every recess I watch him race to the top of the horse chestnut tree with Isaac. It's a rare surprise and something I look forward to: his laughter is clear and strong, ringing out over Pleasant Hill. Oh, be joyful.

After quick worship, I wait for Isaac to cross the lane to go into the left side of the Center Family dwelling. There's just enough moonlight to see him trotting at

Brother John's heels. Isaac is chattering away to Brother John about an East Family calf, one that needs extra milk because it's growing so fast.

I need to know this young man's name. I grasp Isaac's shirtsleeve. "I need to talk to you."

He squirms in my grasp. "I'm not supposed to talk to you."

"Of course you can talk to me. I'm your sister!"

Who's been filling his head with such nonsense?

"I'm only supposed to talk to Ma. That's what Eldress Mary said, when we first came to Pleasant Hill."

I say bitterly, "She's not coming back. That means you talk to me now."

Isaac sits down in the middle of the lane and starts to cry. I sit down next to him, not caring about dirt on my Shakeress whites. He cries harder.

Isaac, I'm sorry I was angry.

All I can do is wait for him to stop.

"I want Ma," he sobs.

I throw pebbles at the men's staircase to the Center Family dwelling. A kind sister would tell her brother to keep hoping—Ma will be here soon. But I know it in my bones: Ma is not coming back for us. She's missed Easter, and my birthday, and Isaac's, and Baby Anne's. She's not coming back.

Sister Agnetha crosses the lane to the Center Family dwelling. Her face darkens from concern to puzzlement to outrage. I can guess what she's thinking: Why is this boy sobbing as though his heart is broken, in Heaven's perfection on Earth? Of course she doesn't speak to him.

His crying shortens to gasps. I put my hand on his shoulder.

He sniffs. "I'm only supposed to talk to Ma."

"I need your help. What's his name?" I whisper. "The boy you climb the horse chestnut tree with."

"Don't touch me. I'm not supposed to talk to girls."

"You can talk to me. Ask Brother John if you don't believe me. Find out his name and let me know, hear?"

Isaac looks at me, startled. "Rosemary Elizabeth, why do you want to know his name?"

"I . . . he's . . . I just do."

"Are you sweet on him?" Isaac's mouth drops open. "You're not supposed to be sweet on him. Shakers aren't supposed to be sweet on anybody."

"Just find out his name. . . . Isaac, this war can't last forever. When it ends, Ma will fetch us or we'll fetch her. I promise, the three of us will find her."

This night I have another dream about Ma. She's iron-yoked to heavy, sloshing milk buckets, and her face is dirty and streaked with sweat. Sweat is dripping off her chin and splashing onto her ragged clothes. She can barely stand, her iron yoke is so heavy.

I open my eyes to a gray false dawn. Across from me is the soft, slow breathing of sleep—Sister Jane and Sister Lucy. I whisper to my dream Ma, "Where are you? Why won't you fetch us? Isaac and Baby Anne are changing so fast. Don't you miss them? Don't you miss me?"

It is only later, in the Sisters' Waiting Room, with my eyes closed again, that I remember another person from the dream. It was Pa, sitting in my mother's rocker, glaring at me in triumph.

As I sit in the Sisters' Waiting Room, for thirty minutes before each meal and for thirty minutes after, I've been writing a letter to Ma in my head. A constant letter, but it changes all the time.

Ma, did you choose Pa over us? Where are you? Isaac thinks it's wrong to talk to me, and he hasn't seen Baby Anne in weeks. How can he think his own sisters are imperfections?

I visit Baby Anne every day between kitchen chores and the nooning broad grace. She's not a baby anymore. She's standing up, with help. Her first tooth has come in. Don't you want to see her first step?

She'll be walking away from us, from you, before you know it.

6

Hospitality

July 1862

"Snuff that lantern!"

"It's snuffed, you thievin' scalawag."

"Who you callin' scalawag, when your pockets is stuffed with swag?"

"Pipe down! Heed yonder window. I seen a light. Pipe down!"

"Where're them chickens?"

"Them chickens is long gone. We hain't the first to come through here."

"Cease your cackle! Pipe down!"

"Don't tell me to pipe down, you squirrel-eatin' son of a —"

In the girls' side of the Center Family dwelling, Sister Jane whispers, "It's more soldiers, more soldiers in Pleasant Hill. Everyone, wake."

Sister Agnetha is in our retiring room. She shines a lantern right into my face and roughly shakes my shoulder. "The world's people are here, Sister Bess. All of you: Arise and attend them."

"How many this time?" Sister Lucy asks with a yawn.

"More than usual," I say. "Sounds like both Yankees and Rebels."

I wonder what time it is. Surely I haven't been sleeping for more than a few hours.

In fits and starts, and then in a mighty stream, footsore and starving Union and Confederate troops have poured into Pleasant Hill this July. They've taken to sneaking through the back gates these summer nights. Maybe they realize Shakers don't have watchdogs to bark an alarm.

I wonder whether Mother Ann Lee would consider watchdogs an imperfection during wartime.

Instead, we have Sister Agnetha. Her ears could pick up the sound of a fox stealing into a henhouse.

The soldiers all tell us the same story. On July 10 none other than Confederate officer John Hunt Morgan himself called on the men of the Bluegrass to "rise and arm, and drive the Hessian invaders from our soil." He and his Raiders occupied Lebanon, Kentucky, two days later. Union troops garrisoned there fled south into Tennessee, or northeast to Lexington. On July 17, Morgan raided Cynthiana, Kentucky, and again Union troops fled either south or west.

The ones that fled west ended up here, with Rebels in hot pursuit.

All summer long, both armies have considered Pleasant Hill a rallying point and foraging stop. Our spring vegetable gardens have been stripped bare. The brethren have chased soldiers out of the henhouses. Lately the brethren have taken turns standing watch over our orchards and pastures.

After a bevy of soldiers from Cut and Shoot, Texas, fired their rifles at Elder Benjamin on July 4, the Shakers decided they had to do something to stave off the stealing. They set up long tables in front of the Trustee's Office. The lesser chores are ignored for now; we share our bounty with all comers.

Twice a day, the tables groan with platters of food. There is plenty for all. The soldiers may eat their fill, but cannot take anything with them.

Elder Benjamin always greets the officers. He doesn't ask them where they're from, and they don't tell him where they're going. He leads them to the understanding that Pleasant Hill is a way station only. The present wave of starving, footsore soldiers must roll out in order for the next wave of even hungrier, more footsore soldiers to roll in.

Sister Agnetha always wakes the school sisters to welcome the soldiers and to charm them into their best behavior. The brethren are fearful for their youngest, who might be conscripted as drummer boys, or so I've heard; the schoolboys sleep through it all and stay away from the tables by day. The Shaker sisters stay away entirely.

Lucky for us, the peaches in the orchards aren't ripe for plucking yet.

The soldiers' uniforms are so blackened with grime and gunsmoke, it's hard to tell who's who. Who's a Billy

Yank? Who's a Johnny Reb? But the Shakers don't care who they are. They're hungry, tired men in dire need of creature comforts and hospitality. That's enough.

What they're not allowed to do on Sinai's Holy Plain is continue the fight. As soldiers line up to eat, Elder Benjamin insists that weaponry and fightin' words stay with the baggage.

The men are so hungry and tired, they're happy to oblige.

Sister Agnetha gives me a hard push out the women's side door. The trunks of the cherry trees shine a ghostly white in the moon's shed light. Already there are soldiers bedding down in the orchards.

"Gentlemen!" I call out into the darkness. "Welcome to Pleasant Hill. We'll serve all of you a good breakfast at dawn. There's good sweet water in the water house, just behind us. You'll find buckets around the water house steps. Help yourselves, and good night. Welcome to Sinai's Holy Plain."

As always, the men jump as high as grasshoppers in a hot skillet when they see me. I reckon I must look like a ghost, with my white nightgown and white sleeping cap.

When I hear the splash of water in the buckets, I know I can go back to sleep.

It's in the treatment of these soldiers that I see the awkward legacy of Mother Ann Lee in full. Her marriage was a trial and an ordeal, or so I've heard in whispers to that effect. She learned to dislike and to distrust men. But the soldiers expect hospitality and Southern charm; we school sisters have been given that task in the food lines.

At dawn the brethren bring food, plates, and cutlery out from the kitchens. The soldiers eat what we eat: Shaker applesauce, steamed dried peaches, herbal tea, cornbread soaked in cream, our own honey, and fruit pies.

"You're a sight for sore eyes, Missy," one soldier tells me as I spoon my very own applesauce onto his plate. "We're much obliged to you Shakers."

"Y'all are angels," another says. "Y'all even look like angels."

Another soldier speaks up. "I've been growing Shaker seed corn, pumpkins, and squash on my farm in Sunbury, Indiana, for years now. The seed packages come in the mail. None finer for my money."

"We've been on the run since Cynthiana," another says. His hands are so grimy I see black fingerprints on the rim of his plate. "This is the first meal we've had since we skedaddled out of Lebanon. How many days is that, Sam—five?"

Sam wedges some cornbread into his mouth. His words are muffled. "Six days. Nothin' but watercress in our bellies since Lebanon, Kentucky."

"I'm glad we can help you," I reply. "Please eat your fill."

After eating a starving man's fill, each soldier wanders back to his bedroll in the orchards to sleep off breakfast. With their caps on their faces and canteens within easy reach, most of them sleep till late afternoon.

Their officers arrive on horseback. The brethren pasture the horses in the North Family's acres. While the officers eat, then sleep in the orchards, the brethren fill the watering troughs again and again. By late morning every army horse lies on its side under the spreading Kentucky coffee shade trees, sleeping deeply. I've never seen such a thing: one hundred horses all lying down at once. The Shaker horses sniff at the army horses curiously but don't disturb them.

Sides of beef and a dozen plucked chickens appear on the kitchen doorstep. The kitchen sisters open jars and jars of last year's summer vegetables. The kitchen sisters prepare great vats of beef and chicken burgoo for when the soldiers wake up.

For a Kentucky burgoo, whatever's on hand goes into the pot: vegetables both root and fresh, fowl, skinned and gutted varmints, shelled nuts, wild greens, canned fruit and vegetables, and wild berries. A Shaker burgoo has just beef or just chicken; the meat is seasoned with salt, pepper, and a few onions and cooked in its own juices. Just like everything from a Shaker kitchen, the burgoo tastes clean, pure, and delicious. Carrots simmered in maple syrup and turnips braised in butter and parsley round out the meal.

The sun is just beginning to set when we school sisters ladle up chicken or beef burgoo for the soldiers' second feeding.

I hold my breath as a new sister, Sister Hannah, staggers up to join us behind the serving tables. Sister Hannah doesn't look to be much older than me. She's not in the school, or in the kitchen, or in the Children's Order. The loose Shaker clothes don't hide her belly, great with child.

Sister Hannah always looks hot, exhausted, and unsteady on her feet.

We have, all of us, noticed she doesn't wear a wedding ring.

The men string out into a long line, metal bowls and spoons at the ready.

"I want to thank you Shaker gals for coming out and feeding us," a soldier remarks to me with a grin.

"They've come out to spark us because we Georgians are so charming!" another soldier shouts.

"Who's that in the front of the line, claiming Georgians are so charming?" a shockingly young man calls out. He reminds me of Isaac, he's so young.

"None more charming than Ohioans," another man returns.

"Miss, you haven't been charmed until you've met a Pilot Grove Missourian. We charm the birds right out of the trees in Pilot Grove."

"You ain't been charmed until you've been charmed by a man from Stockholm, Minnesota."

"A Greenwood, Mississippi, man can charm the whiskers off a catfish."

"A Greenwood, Mississippi, man *looks* like a catfish!"

"Catfish? You must be referring to men from Islamorada, Florida."

I expect the men to start fisticuffing then and there. Instead, they laugh together regardless of where they're from. They all look at us expectantly, with big grins on their grimy faces, eager to flirt with pretty girls, I reckon, despite our Shakeress clothes.

Sister Lucy smiles. "The Shaker sisters are in the kitchens cooking for y'all."

I ladle beef burgoo onto a soldier's plate. It teeters slightly. His left arm is gone, cut clean away at the elbow.

"Miss, I'd be most obliged if I could come back for the carrots and the turnips." His voice has the soft, sweet drawl of a western North Carolinian.

"Of course." I smile at him. For once I feel like explaining. "We're not really Shakers," I say. "We're the girls who live among them here."

Instantly, I wish I could take my words back, for disappointment settles like a blanket thrown over these men. Shoulders and moustaches droop, eyes cloud over.

A man with an aristocratic Tidewater Virginia accent says, "Am I to understand that your charming company is in their stead? That's entirely inhospitable and indelicate. Discourteous."

Several more murmur in agreement.

"It's confounded unnatural, if'n you ask me," another man says.

"Now, Jake, sure'n your ma taught you not to accept another's hospitality if'n yer goin' to rebuke it upon acceptance."

"We're much obliged, though," Jake mutters. "Miss, would you tell them we're much obliged?"

"Of course I will," I stammer. *Why didn't I keep my mouth shut?* "It's their faith that keeps them separate. They all take the same vow."

The Ohioan grunts. "I grew up in Cleveland, near the

Shakertown of North Union. I thought the Kentucky Shakers might wink at the separation, what with Southern belles and Southern hospitality and all."

I ladle burgoo onto his plate. "The separation is here, too."

The Tidewater Virginian, Jake, and his friend look to the Ohioan. "Y'all seen this confounded foolishness in Ohio?" Jake asks.

"I have. Shakertowns are all over New England and New York, too."

The soldiers shake their heads in disbelief. They don't say much except "thank you" and "much obliged" after that.

How is this perfection?

These soldiers are risking their lives, some of them hundreds and hundreds of miles from home, and Sister Agnetha and Sister Emily and the rest won't even come out to look at them! They won't even wish them good luck and Godspeed. Maybe this is how Yankee Shakers behave, but it's downright inhospitable here in the Bluegrass.

Aren't the Shakers Americans, too?

I've seen the runaways hiding in the West Family's corncrib, waiting for a chance to eat and rest up and then cross the Ohio River to freedom. Pleasant Hill is a stop on the Underground Railroad. In their own way, the Shakers are Unionists.

This is your doing, Mother Ann Lee. All these hurt feelings are on your conscience, not mine.

The soldiers leave after two days' rest and recuperation. As the last one marches out through the gate and back to the world's people, the Shakers work even harder. The sisters, rakes and wicker baskets in hand, rush to the orchards. They pick up trash the men have left behind. They rake the grass around the fruit trees. The brethren whitewash the fences where dirty soldiers leaned, leaving grime and oil stains. They bury what seems like an acre of sewage.

The younger brethren, including the young man who climbs the horse chestnut tree with Isaac, haul tables and chairs back to the main dining room.

Sister Hannah scrubs the metal buckets that were left out for the soldiers near the water house. It's a hot day, and her face is red as a poppy.

Within a few hours there's no sign that entire regiments were here, except for the half-empty chicken coops and a half dozen fewer short-horn cattle in the fields.

Sister Agnetha leans against her rake with a groan. "We're in perfect, heavenly order again, leastwise until the next batch of soldiers makes an appearance. I'll pray to Mother for fewer men next time."

"That man from the Tidewater told us that Colonel Augustus Wilford has died," I say. "The colonel was such a gallant gentleman. I saw his tintype once in a Lexington newspaper. He was from Richmond and every inch a soldier."

"I saw Colonel Augustus Wilford on horseback once," Sister Jane pipes up. "He looked so dashing and brave." She sighs. "It's so sad."

Sister Agnetha looks at Sister Jane sharply. "Hearts to

God. And the rest of you school sisters as well. Hands to work, hearts to God."

Sister Jane blushes. "Yes, Sister Agnetha."

We go back to work.

In quick worship tonight, the sisters and brethren sing and dance together, but on opposite sides of the Meetinghouse. We sing and dance in a long snake looping back on itself. The dance is called the Endless Chain.

We dance again to the Wheel Dance, the women in the middle and the men on the edge, around and around the floor.

Each time soldiers take their leave, the Shakers sing this song, to celebrate that their heavenly order is in place once again:

> "Come life, Shaker life, come life eternal,
> Shake, shake out of me all that is carnal.
> Come life, Shaker life, come life eternal,
> Shake, shake out of me all that is carnal.
> I'll take nimble steps. I'll be a David.
> I'll show Michael twice how he behaved."

The young man I've admired in the horse chestnut tree dances right past. The second time I glance at him, he winks.

7

Winter Shakers

It's been nearly six months since Ma left us. Isaac, Baby Anne, and I remain at Pleasant Hill.

I still talk to Isaac after every nooning. It's clear he's happy here, on Sinai's Holy Plain, and I know why. Pa does not stumble home at dawn, roaring drunk and cursing the names of Abraham Lincoln and General Ulysses Simpson Grant.

Even if I have to stay with my siblings at Pleasant Hill for the rest of my life, even if we have to turn ourselves inside out to reach Shaker perfection, I never want Baby Anne to be so terrorized again.

Isaac's eyes are clear, no longer clouded with worry and dread. He hasn't spoken about Ma in a week. I don't know whether this is a good thing or a bad thing.

"I think about Ma all the time," I say on a steaming July afternoon. We share the iron bench in front of the Trustee's Office. We've long since stopped waiting at the front gate of Pleasant Hill. "Do you?"

"I miss her." Isaac holds up his left foot. "Sister Bess! Look! New Believer shoes."

"Where did you get those?"

Isaac smiles. "Brother John made them just for me. He knows everything about shoemaking! And beekeeping, and cabinetmaking, and glassmaking. He's our schoolmaster, too. Brother John says I'm a fast learner and he's going to teach me everything he knows."

My brother has a real father at last.

"I'm glad you're so happy, Isaac. But you don't have to call me Sister Bess. I *am* your sister."

Isaac's eyes cloud with worry. "I'll have to ask Brother John."

"Ask him!"

"Yes, Sister Bess."

"Rosemary Elizabeth Lipking. Say it, Isaac. Say, 'My sister, Rosemary Elizabeth Lipking.'"

Isaac looks around and then whispers, "'My sister, Rosemary Elizabeth Lipking.'"

"Isaac, talking to your own sister is not an imperfection."

"You should call me Brother Isaac."

I stare at him in amazement. "What are you taking about? You *are* my brother, Isaac. You're Baby Anne's brother, too."

Isaac does not look persuaded. "I'm only supposed to talk to Ma."

"Talking in front of the Trustee's Office is fine. Sister Agnetha said so."

Isaac smiles up at me. "Do you like her?"

I like to see him smile, so I grin back. "I'm glad you and Brother John get along so well."

I no longer dream about Ma or Pa. I don't know whether this is a good thing or a bad thing. Instead, I dream about the Shaker horses in the North Family's pasturage. They're running, or kicking up their heels, or springing straight up, twisting and whinnying, tossing their manes and tails.

The Kentucky thoroughbreds among them slow-trot in an easy, airy circle, round and round. In deep-throated nickers, the horses call and respond to one another across Pleasant Hill's pastures.

I wake up puzzled.

Ma likes King Nebuchadnezzar's dreams, in the Book of Daniel, but her favorites are in the Book of Genesis, where Joseph interpreted Pharaoh's dreams. "Dreams are our heart's desire or what we're most afraid of," she likes to say. "Ponder on your dreams, and you'll find the answers you seek."

Why am I dreaming about horses running loose in the pastures?

It is now Sister Amy's task to peel apples.

I break eggs all morning long. What with two eggs each for breakfast, and another two or so eggs each for cakes, molasses brown bread, pies, and puddings, the five hundred Pleasant Hill Shakers eat more than two thousand eggs a day.

I break each egg into a small bowl, sniff it for age, then add it to a larger bowl. Before the eggs reach me, it's someone else's task to candle them—to look for fertilized eggs, with chicks already growing inside them. Fertilized eggs are tucked back under hens to hatch.

I've broken thousands of eggs and not found one chick within. I've never smelled a bad egg, either.

Daily the North Family brethren dry and crush the mountain of eggshells between Kentucky limestone mill wheels. They add the crushed shells to the chicken feed to strengthen the eggs, and to garden soil to sweeten it for next year's harvest. They use crushed eggshells for mortar, to strengthen the cement for the stone-wall root cellars and basements.

Nothing goes to waste at Pleasant Hill.

Egg breaking is considerably easier than apple peeling. With apples I had to pay attention to the paring knife in my hand. As I break eggs, my mind wanders.

On Mr. Godfrey's dairy farm, after my chores were finished for the day, I was allowed to look through the Godfrey library. I could read any book I wanted as long as I didn't take it home. That was fine with me—Mr. Godfrey's library was quiet and the light was better than in our log cabin.

It is Mrs. Godfrey who is addicted to novels. She has them shipped special, all the way from Newport News, Virginia. Some of her books were printed in London, England, and Edinburgh, Scotland. I used to sniff the pages and try to smell the salty ocean air. I'd marvel at the British spellings—*colour* and *humour*.

Mrs. Godfrey is so kind: she taught me to read and then opened their library to me. In the late afternoon we had literary tea parties in her Sunday parlor. We talked about our favorite novelists and our favorite characters. Mrs. Godfrey always poured store-bought tea and served Cassandra's fruit scones with plenty of the butter I'd churned for her.

She never minded if I took scones home for Isaac.

Sir Walter Scott's *Ivanhoe* and *The Tale of Old Mortality*, Jonathan Swift's *Gulliver's Travels*, Daniel Defoe's *Robinson Crusoe* and *Moll Flanders*, James Fenimore Cooper's Leatherstocking series, anything by William Makepeace Thackeray, and anything by Jane Austen or the Brontë sisters—I'd read and read and couldn't wait until I could start the next chapter.

When Pa was especially bad, I would take comfort from King Richard, the Lady Rowena, and Rebecca of York; Elizabeth Bennet and Mr. Darcy; Hawkeye and Cora, Chingachgook, and Uncas; Moll Flanders; Catherine Earnshaw; Jane Eyre; and the Lady Lyndon. I'd pretend the heroines were my older sisters, and they'd encourage me to be as strong as they. "Consider all my hardships and I survived," each seemed to say.

If I had time to think about them, those heroines could help me here at Pleasant Hill. Maybe I should ask to break eggs all the time.

The best heroines aren't perfect, I realize suddenly. Pride, prejudice, selfishness, hypocrisy, and weakness make heroines more like real people. Sometimes they seem more real than my own family.

Heroines aren't like the Shakers, not one bit.

I crack eggs and think about home.

When Pa wasn't there, Ma, Isaac, and I would eat supper together and laugh over funny or interesting things that had happened that day. Once a flock of redbirds landed behind our cabin, hundreds of them. Just as mysteriously, they took off again as one, their red feathers against the evergreens as cheery as Christmas.

We talked about it for days. Where were they going? Why did they land on Mr. Godfrey's dairy farm? What were they looking for? Did they find it?

A kitchen sister, Sister Ruth, shakes my arm. "Did you hear me, Sister Bess?" She places an enormous white bowl on the counter. "I asked for two hundred eggs. I'm to make fifty Ohio lemon pies for tonight's supper."

"I'm sorry; I wasn't listening."

"Daydreaming is an imperfection," she says briskly. "Hands to work."

"Yes, Sister."

These Shakers, smiling innocently as they work, removed from a world they left gladly. No wonder they think Pleasant Hill is so pleasant; they've abandoned family troubles and a nation at war on the other side of these trim Kentucky fences. *Oh, be joyful*—but safety has a price.

In my mind, I'm still writing that same letter to Ma, just changing the words. I can count two hundred eggs and write my letter at the same time.

Ma, Isaac and Baby Anne are leaving us. In the spring I made Isaac promise to be perfect. I don't understand how, because I scarcely have time to think, but that relentless Shaker perfection is pulling us away from you.

*

As I leave the kitchen to wash before the nooning, Sister Emily blocks my way. "Sister Ruth asked for two hundred eggs. Thee gave her a bowl with one hundred and eighty-nine eggs."

"I'm sorry, Sister Emily."

Sister Emily puts her hands on her hips. "Sister Ruth said thee was daydreaming. Woolgathering. Is that why thee miscounted, Sister Bess?"

"It won't happen again. I'm sorry."

The next afternoon I'm in the girls' school ground. Isaac and the young man who winked at me during the Wheel Dance are climbing the horse chestnut tree again. I watch them, as do the spring lambs. The lambs are much bigger than in April, but they still like to watch the climbers.

Isaac's voice rings out over the still air of Pleasant Hill, as loud as the four-thirty morning bell. "Rosemary Elizabeth! Rosemary Elizabeth!"

I freeze, for it seems as though every Shaker has paused to listen.

In their garden, members of the East Family cease tending, their rakes and hoes in the air. They've stopped to stare at us school sisters and brethren.

Sister Agnetha is staring out the school window right at me, her eyes wide in shock.

The Pleasant Hill blacksmith and stonemason is an ex-slave from Virginia, Freeman Thomas Jones. He pokes his head out of the forge to stare. The broom makers in the broom shop, the weavers and dyers in the cloth shop, the butter and cheese makers in the dairy, the carpenters in the woodcraft shop, the wheel makers in the cooper's shop, and the sisters canning plums in the summer kitchen—each pokes his or her head out of a door in shock and alarm.

All the school sisters have stopped jumping rope, or playing hopscotch, to stare at me.

It's as though Heaven and Earth are standing still, holding their breath, waiting for the thunderstruck imperfection that will forever tear asunder one from the other.

"Rosemary Elizabeth! Rosemary Elizabeth! Where are you?"

"Isaac," I whisper, though he can't possibly hear me from so far away. "Don't say anything more! Please don't say another word! Wait until we meet in front of the Trustee's Office tomorrow." For I know what he's about to shout from one end of Pleasant Hill to another, and the separation of the sexes is the most important perfection at Pleasant Hill.

Even thinking about a young man is an imperfection. I can't begin to imagine the trouble I'm in.

Isaac's voice rings out innocently. "Rosemary Elizabeth! That boy you're sweet on? His name is Brother Daniel. Daniel Frye."

I run up all four floors to the girls' school to hide. On the landing I bump into Sister Agnetha, her arms full of felt chalk erasers. "Go downstairs, stand in the lane, and clean these," she snaps.

I pound erasers as staring Shakers walk by. I might as well be in a pillory, where folks used to be bound hand

and foot and exposed to public ridicule. Clouds of chalk settle on my white clothes. At least the chalk is white; I won't have to change before going back to school.

It was Sister Jane who explained about the winter Shakers. They're folks who stay in a Shakertown for the winter, swearing on their mothers' souls that they fully intend to enter into Covenant with the Believers. As soon as the weather warms, off they fly.

Which are worse, I wonder—the ones who lie to the Shakers or those who lie to themselves?

On my very first day at Pleasant Hill, Sister Agnetha called me a winter Shaker. The Believers treat the winter Shakers with kindness but not with sweet Union. There's a difference. They don't trust winter Shakers.

The school sisters and brothers don't have to swear to anything. We don't have to lie; we're treated as winter Shakers anyway. We're taught the Bible, the history of dissent within the Protestant Reformation, and the teachings of Mother Ann Lee.

It takes five years of study to become a final-stage Shaker. At that point, a newly minted Believer gives everything he or she has to the community: land, inheritance, house, barn, furniture, china, and cutlery—lock, stock, and barrel.

I look in wonder at Sister Emily, Sister Agnetha, and Eldress Mary. To the Shakers, these sisters might as well be angels on Earth. They tread the Shaker path in a state of certain Shaker grace.

But truth be told, sometimes the sisters don't look or

act any more perfect than the rest of us. They can be cranky, petty, and hectoring. That makes us all winter Shakers, I reckon. So who is lying? Who is telling the truth?

I can tell that Sister Agnetha doesn't think much of Sister Emily. Her mouth crimps in disapproval whenever Sister Emily says "thee" instead of "you."

While the rest of us are washing breakfast dishes, when she thinks no one is looking, Sister Emily gulps a second cup of coffee on the kitchen back stoop. I've seen her there when I've gone outside for a breath of air.

And when we have chocolate cake, I've seen Eldress Mary hoarding cakes just for herself, behind some barrels in the icehouse. I've seen her steal into the icehouse after quick worship, with a fork and a plate tucked in her snowy white sleeve.

When I see imperfections among the sisters, I catch the eye of Sister Jane or another school sister and nudge her arm. We smile together, then pretend we didn't see anything amiss.

One evening back in May, the rain poured and the thunder rolled. The school sisters and I ran across the lane and into the Center Family dwelling. We missed quick worship altogether and took our sponge baths early.

In the dim light, a soft glimmer shone around Sister Amy's neck. I exclaimed, "A pearl necklace! I've only seen pearls on Mrs. Godfrey."

Sister Amy gasped and clamped her hands around her neck as the other girls reached for towels and nightgowns. Sister Jane stepped forward. "We never mention home treasures to the sisters, Sister Bess," she said in her calm and firm voice. She wore a silver locket on a chain so delicate I could scarcely see it. "They're to be kept a secret."

"I won't breathe a word to anyone. I wish I had a home treasure."

As I drifted off to sleep, the thunder and rain abated and the roar of quick worship filled my ears. Our neighbors across the Pike hear the quick worship every night; they must wonder what the joyful noise is all about.

Each of the school sisters has something, a keepsake from home. Sister Amy wears the pearl necklace. Sister Patience wears her mother's tortoiseshell hair comb under her Shaker cap. Sister Sarah hides a red satin music box under some floorboards. Sister Lucy has her father's watch fob—a beautiful gold chain with a gilded bear's tooth on one end—nestled in her apron pocket. Sister Jane has her locket.

It's been a shock and a comfort to realize that they don't believe in the Shaker path any more than I do.

We're all waiting for the war to be over, for our parents to collect us, for a chance to live among the world's people once again. How many others who live at Pleasant Hill are waiting for a chance to be winter Shakers no more?

I don't have a treasure from home, except my constant letter to Ma.

Ma, fetch us. Fetch us soon, for I don't know how much longer I can strive toward Shaker perfection. I have to sleep as an angel, flat on my back with my arms folded across my chest. You know how much I like to sleep on my side, curled into a snug ball. Sometimes I think Sister Agnetha pulls my legs down to the bottom of my bed when I'm sleeping. At times I wake suddenly to find my feet touching the bedfoot.

In school Sister Agnetha asks us to describe our angel dreams. I make up my angel dreams, and I'm pretty sure the other school sisters do, too. All of Pleasant Hill can't be dreaming of angels, can they?

All Isaac ever talks about is Brother John and staying here to learn how to be a proper Shaker. Isaac's happy and safe, but at what cost, Ma? Just yesterday he told me that he's trying to use his left hand instead of his right, to step off with his left foot instead of his right, since brethren go to the left in all ways—the left side of the staircase, the left door to the dining room, the left door to the Meetinghouse, the left door to the dwellings, shops, and barns. They walk on the left side of the lanes and footpaths.

Can someone decide to change from right- to left-handed? Will that make him more perfect?

Isaac and Baby Anne are pulling away from me. I feel myself pulling away from myself. I scarcely know who I am anymore.

Ma, it's as though what makes me myself—the Shakers don't want that, whatever it is. Every once in a while I'll see someone's perfection slip, and the real person will shine through: a real person with a hankering for chocolate cake, or kittens, or horses, or a second cup of coffee. The Shakers don't want that shine, but isn't that shine the best part of who we are?

I'm secretly sweet on someone you'd like—Brother Daniel. I dance past him and he smiles at me. But we're not allowed to talk. I can smile back if I'm sure Sister Agnetha isn't watching.

Hurry and fetch us, or we will all be so perfect you won't recognize us.

8

Obadiah

Every day I admire the pastured horses. The Shaker horses are calm, contented, eager to please, and honest as the sunrise. I pluck succulent grass from under the fruit trees and give each horse a mouthful.

One especially, a sweet-tempered gelding named Obadiah, will eat his mouthful and then wait patiently to have his nose stroked. Every day I think of a reason why I need to walk by the East Family's pasture. He watches me with his ears turned forward. He'll welcome me with a deep-throated nicker and give his head a friendly shake in my direction.

Or I'll stand by a fence post and up he'll trot for grass and petting. I talk to him, too, as long as no Shaker can hear me.

I'd gladly work in the stables if the brethren would let me. I've always been good with horses. Mr. Godfrey let me groom his horses—his carriage horse, his plow horse, his horses-out-to-pasture—and all had gleaming coats and shining manes and tails because of me. Good horsemanship is a Kentuckian's birthright. As long as it's understood that a horse is as timid as a mouse but a thousand pounds heavier, working with horses is easy.

But horses are men's work at Pleasant Hill.

Elder Benjamin made an announcement before Wednesday's quick worship. Two cats have found their way into the East Family's cow barn. The brethren tried to shoo them away, but they'd returned by morning.

I said solemnly to Sister Agnetha, "Are there rats and mice in the East Family's cow barn? Surely rats and mice can't be part of Mother Ann Lee's perfect, heavenly order on Earth."

For once, Sister Agnetha had nothing to say, at least to me . . .

. . . but Eldress Mary prayed reverently on the matter. Elder Benjamin prayed gravely on the matter. Two evenings ago, Elder Benjamin announced that the cats could stay. How the two of them reached an agreement when they can't even talk to each other is a mystery I still haven't solved.

Both cats littered, and now kittens are part of the perfect, heavenly order, at least in the East Family's cow barn at Pleasant Hill.

Eldress Mary has volunteered Sister Agnetha to take a season's worth of butter and cheese into Lexington. The Shakers collect cash money from the world's people to buy the goods they can't make or grow: coffee and pekoe tea, needles and thimbles, silk thread, salt and pepper, lemons, nutmeg, cinnamon and chocolate, paper, postage stamps, and raw cotton.

It must be a sister who goes to Lexington. Two of the brethren went last year. They were conscripted into the Union army on the spot, right on the Harrodsburg Pike. Luckily for the Shakers, Obadiah made his way home, still harnessed to the empty buckboard.

I want so much to join her. I haven't been out among the world's people since Ma left us here. It would be a rare treat, even in Sister Agnetha's company, to see the sights of Lexington again.

I stand in front of Sister Agnetha's desk and beg. "I can talk to the world's men, and a final-stage Shakeress can't, Sister Agnetha. Please may I go along?"

"I'm to speak to the wife of Mr. Kettleman. He's a wholesaler. The Believers at Pleasant Hill sell all our butter and cheese to him." Sister Agnetha stacks a row of books with the bound edges perfectly aligned. "The last thing the Believers need is for you to talk to the world's men."

"What?"

"Sister Priscilla saw you laughing with the soldiers. An imperfection."

"But you ordered us to charm them into their best behavior! Kentucky women are known for their warm hospitality. Elder Benjamin has made Pleasant Hill a haven for soldiers. And what about that Shaker song?"

I sing the first lines:

"Gentle words, softly spoken,
often soothe the troubled mind.
While links of love are broken
with words that are unkind."

Sister Agnetha crimps her mouth, shakes her head firmly.

"And . . . I have a gift with horses. Mr. Godfrey trusted me with his carriage and plow horses."

Sister Agnetha is terrified of horses, so this is the better argument. I've been saving it for this moment.

"We'll take Obadiah," I say quickly. "He's a carriage horse. He knows the way home from Lexington. With me there, you won't have to tack him up, or drive him, or graze him, or water him, or brush him down, or clean his hooves, or anything."

The biggest horse pasture is down the hill from the Center Family dwelling. I study Sister Agnetha while she studies the horses through the schoolroom window. What luck! The herd is engaged in horseplay, running around the pasture, kicking up their heels. A horse kicks the fence.

A loud *crack* splits the air.

I give her my last, best argument. "Carriage horses respond best to voice commands. I'll have to talk to Obadiah. An imperfection."

Sister Agnetha smiles thankfully.

Before dawn I hitch Obadiah to a Shaker buckboard. A bevy of brethren hover, like buzzards on a fence rail. I know they're eager to find errors. I stand off to the side for a moment so they can take a good look at how I put a horse under harness. To his credit, Obadiah stands perfectly still.

I tie my sunbonnet under my chin and smile at their disappointment.

As the brethren pack cheese and butter onto chipped ice in the back, I scramble into the driver's seat and pull Sister Agnetha up beside me.

I touch Obadiah's right wither. He walks forward. At the front gate we turn left. As the sun rises, we're on the Pike heading northeast toward Lexington. After a bit, I hear another horse and carriage behind us. It's Brother Daniel in a meadowbrook pulled by Obadiah's dam, Molly.

I reckon Brother Daniel will follow us to Lexington. He wants us to be safe, what with the war on. *An outing with Brother Daniel*—I smile and keep my good cheer to myself.

Sister Agnetha glances behind her once. She squares her shoulders and doesn't look back again.

By late morning it's hot enough to stop by a stream for some water.

Sister Agnetha lays out our food under a Kentucky coffee tree. Brother Daniel holds both horses by the bridles. We eat silently, as though in the dining hall. Surely Brother Daniel is as hungry and thirsty as we are. He doesn't even look in our direction.

I set out a metal drinking cup, some of the salt-cured ham, Shaker sharp cheddar, molasses brown bread, four apples, and two slices of peach pie.

I stand up. "I'm leaving some food here," I announce loudly to Sister Agnetha. "There's plenty of water to drink in the stream. I'll take hold of Obadiah and Molly's bridles, and we'll wait for Brother Daniel to eat his fill. He'd better hurry over, before the ants get wind of the bounty."

Sister Agnetha is a large woman, but she leaps away from the picnic cloth in a single bound. I gather up the bridles from Brother Daniel. Without a word he kneels on the picnic cloth and wolfs down the food. Sister Agnetha sits in the buckboard, staring into space.

"Obadiah, walk on." Despite the heat, the horse steps forward obediently. Obadiah's a Morgan, the very first American horse, bred in Vermont in 1790 by Mr. Justin Morgan. Morgans are strong and smart. Obadiah is as small and well rounded as a Lexington merry-go-round horse, but he's tough as iron. He's been trotting all day, and he's not even sweating.

By midafternoon, Obadiah's dam, Molly, is tired and winded. Her pace slows to a pokey walk. Obadiah lifts his head and nickers to Molly from time to time. She always answers.

Every once in a while I glance over at Sister Agnetha. Finally, when she seems settled, her face no longer so fearful and preoccupied, I decide this is the best time to ask the questions I haven't yet asked in the outhouse line.

"Why do we hold our palms up in the Sisters' Waiting Room? Why do Shakers pray that way?"

Sister Agnetha smiles. "That we may better receive

God's grace. Open palms are a symbol of the Believer's trust and complete surrender."

That was easy—she even seemed happy to answer.

"Why does Sister Emily say *thee*? Nobody else does."

"She grew up a Philadelphia Quaker. Did you know that Mother Ann Lee was a Quaker before she founded the Believers? The world's people called our first order the Shaking Quakers. Sister Emily's *thee*'s are a prideful habit with her, in my opinion."

"Why do the school sisters sing about sweeping the floor every morning?"

She claps her hands. "That's a wonderful story, Sister Bess! When Mother Ann Lee was on her deathbed, a young sister was sweeping the floor on the porch next to her bedroom. Mother pulled herself out of bed, went out onto the porch, and told the sister to sweep the floor well.

"Three times she pulled herself out of her own deathbed, went out onto the porch, and told the young sister to sweep the floor well. The sister understood the deeper meaning: We're to keep our hearts swept clean, in keeping with our perfect, heavenly order, because there is no dirt in Heaven. So every morning the sisters sing the sweeping song as they sweep."

Obadiah snorts. A skeptic, I reckon. I know how he feels.

Everything Mother Ann Lee said has come to have a deeper meaning. Keep the floors swept. Sleep on your back with your arms folded. Don't mush up the apples when making applesauce. Boil the lemon skins, then add that water to make Shaker lemonade. Keep foods separate. Don't talk while eating. Don't have anything to do with men. Shake and shout yourself into a frenzy as you worship.

If female, step off with the right foot on every occasion. Dress the right side of your body first. Hands to work. No pets; no talking to animals. There's nothing worse than dirt. Dirt is an abomination unto the Lord.

No reading for pleasure.

The Shakers have turned Mother Ann Lee's preferences, habits, and prejudices into commandments.

"Is it true your ma left you with the Shakers to run off with a gambling man from New Orleans?"

To my astonishment, Sister Agnetha laughs. I've never heard her laugh before. "Is that the story? Nay, my stepmother had children of her own. After my father died, she left me here. I was just eight years old.

"I thank God every day that she left me at Pleasant Hill. I live in Heaven on Earth. So do you." She pats my hand. "So do you."

The story isn't true! "So . . . your mother didn't abandon you?"

"Sister Bess, the world beyond Pleasant Hill's gates is all confusion. The world's people are bewildered because they lack our perfection. I'm sure your mother loves you dearly—you, Brother Isaac, and Baby Anne. She'll come to her senses.

"Meanwhile, use this time God has given you. The gift to be simple, the gift to be free, held fast along the Believer path. It's how we've achieved heavenly perfection on Earth. We want life to be quiet and in perfect array. We do the same things in the same way, day after day, so our minds are free for sweet Union with God and Mother Ann Lee."

Obadiah trots on. I want to ask her about winter Shakers. Surely she knows about Eldress Mary's chocolate cakes. Does she know about Sister Emily's coffee? Doesn't she know—or at least suspect—that Sister Priscilla and Sister Deborah play with the East Family's barn kittens every afternoon?

Doesn't she see the young sisters and brethren looking at one another during the Wheel Dance at quick worship?

Mother Ann Lee considered beer and spirits a gross imperfection—no surprise there—but I know I've smelled it on the brethren. I know what alcohol smells like on a man.

"Don't you think the Shakers have turned Mother Ann Lee into an idol and abandoned the world?" I ask politely. "That you've abandoned the world and all its problems and complications?"

"Mother Ann Lee is not an idol!" Sister Agnetha says crossly. "'Step out from among them and be ye separate.'" Here she looks at me sharply. "Why do you think we call our towns Heaven on Earth?"

The Harrodsburg Pike fills up with more and more wagons as we approach Lexington. A company of Union soldiers and their officers march by.

An officer holds up two gold coins. His voice is as flat as water in a bucket. "I'll give you forty dollars in United States currency for that horse."

I look back the way we came. Brother Daniel and

Molly are no longer behind us. A soldier reaches for Obadiah's bridle. The gelding shies away and whinnies in panic.

"Mother Lee, be my shield," Sister Agnetha whispers.

"Obadiah! Trot on!" I touch his flank with the whip and give his reins a smart shake. He breaks into a fast trot as the officer curses his disappointment.

"I'm surprised he didn't try to steal him," Sister Agnetha mutters.

"President Lincoln was born in Kentucky."

She gives me a baffled look.

"He would never condone horse thieving."

Eventually, Obadiah slows to an easy, loose-rein trot.

After another hour or so, Sister Agnetha points to a gravel drive with spreading oaks on opposite sides. An iron letter *K* hangs between the trees. "Turn here. This is the Kettleman farm."

Just a slight shift with my left hand turns Obadiah smartly left and into the drive. The brethren have trained him well.

At the end of the long drive are a white farmhouse, an open-air tobacco shed, a barn, a woodshed, a slaughtering shed, some chicken coops, and a warehouse.

I've grown used to Pleasant Hill, where not a board needs painting, not a step needs repairing, not a roof needs shingling, not a window needs replacing, not a garden needs weeding, not a stall needs cleaning, not a fence needs mending.

The Kettleman place is a good farm, but in dire need of repairs.

I see imperfections everywhere! Am I becoming a

Shaker? *It must be the war,* I think sadly. *Either they can't afford to keep the farm up or the materials are not to be had.*

When Mr. Kettleman opens the back of the buckboard, icy water pours forth as a wave.

Apparently, Mr. Kettleman and his wife are used to this arrangement with the Shakers. "Mrs. Kettleman," Sister Agnetha calls out. "Good afternoon, and please wish your husband a good afternoon as well."

"Mrs. Kettleman," Mr. Kettleman answers, "wish Sister Agnetha a good afternoon. I'll buy all these cheese rounds outright. I'm guessing they're ten pounds apiece?"

I look at Sister Agnetha in surprise. "You know them?" I exclaim. "You've been here before?"

She ignores me. "Mrs. Kettleman," Sister Agnetha says, "tell Mr. Kettleman they're fifteen pounds apiece. We kept the stoves going all winter in our barns, and the cows yielded half again as much milk as previous winters thanks to the extra warmth. Our icehouse was filled to bursting with butter and cheese."

"Mrs. Kettleman," Mr. Kettleman says, "tell Sister Agnetha that that's clever, about the stoves. I'll have to remember for my own dairy next winter."

Open-mouthed, Mrs. Kettleman turns her head back and forth, back and forth, as Sister Agnetha and Mr. Kettleman talk past her. It's as though she's watching the school sisters on the schoolyard swings.

Where is Brother Daniel? I don't imagine he's ever been to the Kettlemans' farm before; he must be lost. I hope we meet with him on the way home.

After they've settled on prices and the cheese wheels

and butter blocks are packed in ice in the warehouse, Mrs. Kettleman speaks up. "You must be tired from your journey. I thought we'd have a tea party before your departure. I baked some of my mother's tea cakes special just this morning."

"Thank you so much!" I say quickly, before Sister Agnetha has a chance to refuse. "I'm Rosemary Elizabeth Lipking. A tea party would be lovely."

Mr. Kettleman says to Mrs. Kettleman, "Tell Sister Agnetha I'll unhitch the gelding and lead him to the barn for water, hay, and rest."

I don't look at Sister Agnetha; she probably doesn't want to stay, but it would be rude to snub our hostess. "Thank you, Mr. Kettleman. Obadiah would like that. There's another person in our party. His name is Daniel Frye, and he's driving another Morgan in front of a meadowbrook."

"I'll clean a stall and put down fresh bedding, Miss Lipking."

"Thank you, Mr. Kettleman."

I'll not snub our host, either.

We sit in Mrs. Kettleman's Sunday parlor while a kitchen maid fetches the tea things. The comforting *chink* of china and cutlery rings out from the kitchen. I gaze in wonder at the parlor.

I've grown used to plain, honey-colored furniture and plenty of sunlit space within each room. According to the Shakers, it's all that empty space that invites quiet thoughts and meditations. The modest beauty is serene, pure.

The contrast between the world's people and the Shakers couldn't be starker. Here at the Kettlemans', the Sunday parlor is jammed full with heavy, dark furniture. Mahogany dressers, highboys, tables, curio cabinets, and occasional chairs, all as purple-black as prunes, are crowded together in a room much too small for this amount of furniture.

The parlor makes me feel vexed and fretful, suffocated, as though there's not enough air to breathe.

To my surprise, Brother Daniel walks in. He doesn't say a word, but doffs his Shaker hat to the ladies as a Southern gentleman will do. What took him so long? Is Molly lame? Did the Union soldiers on the Pike give him trouble? I mustn't ask—not unless I want an earful from Sister Agnetha on our trip back to Pleasant Hill.

He sits down, his hat on his knee, his hands jammed into his pockets and his eyes downcast, on an upholstered settee overstuffed to bursting. The wood trim on the settee seems alive, crawling with tangled vines and dark, thorn-infested thickets. Hawk and eagle talons grip fiercely onto the four legs.

The Sunday parlor is chaotic with knickknacks: dusty feathers, pocketbooks, baskets, colored eggs, birds' nests, tiny daguerreotypes in dark wooden frames, seashells, newspapers, maps to the Mammoth Cave, and embroidered table mats and screens. Paintings cloak the walls, the landscapes so dark and muddy it's hard to know what the artists intended. Their frames are dark and vine-entangled, too.

It sounds peculiar, but all the furniture and clutter, all

these bits and pieces, tell me too much about the Kettlemans. Shaker rooms reveal nothing about the interests and habits of the people who live in them. Is that a good thing or a bad thing?

I hadn't noticed until now just how serene and soothing the empty Shaker rooms are—my soul expands with every breath I take there. Am I becoming a Shaker?

The housemaid wheels in a tea cart. The lady of the house pours out and passes round a pretty plate. "The recipe for these Virginia tea cakes has been in my mother's family for a hundred years. She was a Randolph on her mother's side and a member of the First Families of Virginia."

"We can't stay long," Sister Agnetha announces.

I steal a glance at Sister Agnetha. She's glaring at me and tapping her foot in impatience.

I won't be rude. Here among the world's people, that would be an imperfection. I give Sister Agnetha a broad smile and return to my tea.

Mrs. Kettleman serves us tea, cakes, and small talk. Brother Daniel drinks tea, eats cakes, and says nothing. I feel sorry for him. He can't talk to us, and Mrs. Kettleman knows the Shaker customs. She doesn't talk to him.

The tea cakes are a delicate brown, crisp and delicious, with a hint of vanilla and nutmeg. The tea is Lady Jane Grey; the delicate scents of Assam tea, oranges, and bergamot fill my nose with every sip. It's impossible to get English tea in wartime. Mrs. Kettleman must have been saving this tea for a special occasion.

It makes me sad and angry that this awkward tea party is her special occasion.

To break the silence, I ask Mrs. Kettleman if she has any news about the war. She speaks carefully of Union victories in Virginia and Tennessee, and she tells us of Belle Boyd, an alleged Confederate spy who might be released from the Old Capitol Prison in Washington City for lack of evidence.

I can't tell which side she supports, and she's being careful because she doesn't know about me, either.

This is the way it is in Kentucky: We're a slave state *and* a Union state. In churches, in stores, in a stranger's parlor, we never voice opinions unless we're absolutely sure to whom we're speaking.

As Mrs. Kettleman talks, I look around the Sunday parlor for anything that might reveal her allegiance. Mrs. Kettleman's maid is white. That doesn't mean the Kettlemans have no slaves, though.

I spy a tiny stars-and-bars flag on the mantelpiece, but it might be Mr. Kettleman's, not hers. Husbands and wives don't always agree on this war.

For hospitality's sake, I ask my questions graciously. I don't want to give offense to my hostess.

Mr. Kettleman comes in and sits. As he takes tea, he and his wife speak of farm doings in hushed, embarrassed tones. Brother Daniel eats cakes and stares at his feet. All on his own, he gets up and refills his teacup. We watch him sit down again.

"It'll be twilight soon," Sister Agnetha says. "We shouldn't tarry, Sister Bess." She stands up immediately.

"Mrs. Kettleman, would you ask Mr. Kettleman if we might leave our money here again this year? Some of our brethren will come by next week to receive it."

Mrs. Kettleman speaks up. "Land sakes, where are my manners? Of course y'all must all stay the night. We've plenty of room."

"Since entering into the final stage of Covenant, I've not spent one night anyplace but Pleasant Hill," Sister Agnetha whispers loudly to me. Of course the Kettlemans hear her.

"It'll be dangerous out on the Pike. The war," Mr. Kettleman says.

I stretch my mouth into what I hope is a polite smile. "Thank you so much for your offer, Mrs. Kettleman, but we must be on our way. You've shown us so much hospitality. Your mother's tea cakes are delicious. We're much obliged for your kindness."

Mr. Kettleman and Brother Daniel bring Obadiah and Molly from the barn. They hitch them to the buckboard and the meadowbrook again. Molly's head droops. She's tired, and the heat has not yet loosened its grip on the day.

I commence to climb into the buckboard. Mr. Kettleman leans forward. He's a gentleman; I know his impulse is to help me climb up onto the driver's box. Mrs. Kettleman puts a hand on his arm and shakes her head sadly.

Once I'm settled, Sister Agnetha puts out her hand; I give it a sharp yank to pull her up beside me.

"We'll see you next year, Miss Lipking," Mr. Kettleman says. "Thank you for coming. Tell Sister Agnetha we'll see her next year. Take care on the Pike."

"I will. Good day, Mr. and Mrs. Kettleman. Obadiah, walk on."

As we leave, I hear Brother Daniel and the Kettlemans talking. And laughing! The Kettlemans' laughter sounds friendly, welcoming, and hospitable.

Brother Daniel laughs with them—that clear, strong laugh of his.

Being out among the world's people again makes me realize what I've been missing. The company of decent, honest men—where is the imperfection in that?

I missed the perfect opportunity to talk to Daniel Frye, as well.

Sister Agnetha has spoiled my outing to Lexington. A tea party in Lexington with a Virginia hostess, and she's spoiled it.

And once again, she's vexed with me about something.

Sister Agnetha scowls at me as Obadiah clops cheerfully down the Pike.

9

More of the World's People

I touch Obadiah's flanks with the driving crop. He lifts into a fast trot. "Good boy, trot on. It's well we brought a lantern with us," I say to Sister Agnetha. "It'll be dark before we reach Pleasant Hill."

Sister Agnetha says crossly, "You shouldn't have spoken to Mr. Kettleman while dressed as a Believer. It was an unseemly imperfection, especially when you spoke about Brother Daniel."

"You've woken me out of a sound sleep so I could speak to the world's soldiers in my nightgown," I snap back.

"This war is among the world's people," she replies primly. "A Believer needn't think anything about it, or about the world's soldiers."

"How can you *not* think about it? Men are dying!"

"A Believer sister never raises her voice."

I've heard you raise yours every hour of every day.

I say softly, "I've heard the whisperings. I've seen the lanterns at night, and the folks hiding in the West Family's corncrib. I know Pleasant Hill is a stop on the Underground Railroad. You do want the Union to win this war."

Sister Agnetha stares at me. For once she has nothing to say—but just for a moment. "Only God knows how this war will end; that's all we need think about it."

"Because soldiers are men? These men are dying. The Kettlemans offered us hospitality, and you were rude to both of them. Where does it say religion allows a body to be rude?"

"I forget you're a winter Shaker," Sister Agnetha mutters, crosser still.

The humid August night is alive with singing crickets and shrilling tree frogs. A ghostly mist wraps around the tree trunks.

Who is rude now, Miss Rosemary Elizabeth Lipking? Especially after going on and on about Southern hospitality? The Shakers have been more than hospitable to you, to your brother, to your sister.

After a few miles, I ask politely, "How do you know the Kettlemans?"

"I've been there many times with Eldress Mary."

I can only gape in astonishment.

"Eldress Mary is an accomplished horsewoman. She grew up in a big house on the ocean side of New Bedford, Massachusetts, with ballet lessons, a private tutor, and birthday garden parties with a hired orchestra amid the roses." Sister Agnetha's voice is tight with bitterness. "Her

105

father was in commerce and insured merchant ships for a pretty penny."

"Did you know her?" I ask, breathless.

"I grew up on the railroad side of New Bedford."

"So you knew her!"

"Only by her family name." Sister Agnetha twists her mouth. She must think she's said too much. "You think I'm a rude Yankee woman with no respect for Southern sensibilities. I have no manners."

"I didn't say that."

"But you think it."

"I didn't mean to offend you, Sister Agnetha. I'm sorry." The full moon hangs above us, flooding the Pike with silver light. The trees are twinkling the palest green from thousands of fireflies. Obadiah slows to a walk. "We won't need our lantern after all."

"Mother Ann Lee has offered you a precious gift, and you cast it aside as nothing more than bad manners."

I'm angry, but I look behind me and speak in a calm, measured voice, as though I'm still at Mrs. Kettleman's tea party. "We've lost Brother Daniel and Molly, which would never have happened if he'd ridden with us. It's dangerous for two women to be alone at night, especially with the war on. We should have accepted Mrs. Kettleman's kind offer, and not just because she was being hospitable."

Sister Agnetha crosses her arms. "You call us Shakers: yet another imperfection. The United Society of Believers in Christ's Second Appearing do *not* call ourselves Shakers. That is a derogatory name given to us by the world's people."

"That's not true! You call yourselves Shakers." I sing in a loud voice:

"Come life, Shaker life, come life eternal,
Shake, shake out of me all that is carnal. . . ."

Sister Agnetha scowls. "I'm sorry you don't like our perfect, heavenly order. I thought better of you, Sister Bess. Most girls are so silly. You can read and figure. I thought you had a future with the Believers."

I look at her, shocked. "You thought I wanted to stay?"

She looks at me, shocked. "You don't want to be a perfect angel in Heaven on Earth?"

She stares at me. I stare at her. Sister Agnetha leans away from me, her mouth a perfect, horrified O.

Suddenly, a man on horseback gallops up from a hollow alongside the Harrodsburg Pike. "Evening, ladies," he says. He calls like a hoot owl once, twice, thrice. Men on horseback gallop out of the forests on both sides of the Pike.

Mr. Kettleman was right! "Obadiah, trot on!" I shout. As he moves forward, another horse and rider pull up in front of us. Obadiah halts and tosses his head. His feet move uncertainly beneath him. Another rider dismounts and grabs hold of his bridle. Our gelding whinnies and rears up.

"Whoa, boy," the man says in a silky voice. "Easy, little fella. Easy now."

The leader among them tips his hat. "Ladies? We need the horse."

"Nay, you can't have Obadiah." Sister Agnetha's voice

quavers like a turkey gobble. She stands up in the carriage. "He's not for sale."

Obadiah continues to whinny and rear. The buckboard rocks.

The men laugh.

"Ma'am?" another man crows. "We're not buyin' him!"

"Shakers, are you?" A man dismounts and commences to shake as though struck by the palsy. More horses whinny and rear up. The men who are still mounted laugh with gusto.

What can I do?

"Sister Agnetha, sit down!" I shout. "You'll fall!"

"He's not for sale," Sister Agnetha cries out again, her voice trembling.

Their leader dismounts and aims a pistol right between Sister Agnetha's eyes. He says flatly, "Ma'am? We're taking the gelding."

Sister Agnetha squares her shoulders and glares at the pistol barrel. She makes an odd sound, clutches at her chest, and then topples off the buckboard.

"Sister Agnetha?" I jump down and bend over her.

Sister Agnetha lies on the Harrodsburg Pike, staring at up at Heaven with sightless eyes.

"She's dead," I say breathlessly. She hasn't spoken to a man in thirty years—that and a highwayman's pistol pointed at her. She's dead. "You scared her to death!"

One of the men asks, "Where're you from, miss? Where're yer folks? You hain't no Shaker."

"Mr. Godfrey's dairy farm," I stammer. *How can she be dead?* "Ma left us. I don't know where's Pa."

The men whoop and holler at that. "Maybe you're from Indiana?" one calls out. "The Hoosier State. 'Who's yer Pa? Who's yer Pa?'" he crows.

"Enough!" the leader shouts. The men stop laughing instantly. "Miss, you tell the Shakers that this fine Morgan has been donated to the Cause."

They ease Obadiah out of his traces. A young highwayman cuts most of the driving reins off with a knife. He ties the ends together for makeshift riding reins. They ignore Sister Agnetha's body.

"This is a Pleasant Hill Shakeress," I splutter. "You can't just leave her here. You can't just leave Sister Agnetha on the Harrodsburg Pike."

A man steps forward. "You're from Pleasant Hill? Would you say hello to my daughter, Ellen Hall?"

"Sister Patience?" *Sister Agnetha is dead, Obadiah is stolen, I'm to be kidnapped by highwaymen, and Sister Patience's father is making polite conversation!* "I . . . I know your daughter, Mr. Hall. I eat every meal with her. She's in school with me. She loves kittens."

"Y'all have enough vittles for the winter? Is Ellen happy? Is she doing her lessons? School was always a trial for her. She'd stare out the window and pay no attention to the teacher. Always dreamy—"

This is madness! "I—I reckon she's happy, Mr. Hall. She's out of the war."

"That she is." Mr. Hall pushes a wooden box—about the size of a woodchuck—into my hands. "This is for you and Ellen. Good luck, miss."

What can I do? "Thank you."

Their leader leans toward me. "What's your name?" he demands.

I pull back. "Rosemary Elizabeth Lipking," I whisper.

"What kind of name is Lipking?"

More polite conversation? I blink at him in surprise. "It's . . . Norwegian. My grandparents were born in Stavanger, Norway."

He studies me as I study him. His gray eyes are full of mocking high spirits, as though we share a joke between us.

"I suspect it's cold in Norway. The Lipkings are used to the cold?"

"My grandparents always said Norwegians are hearty folk."

He turns to his followers. "Men! This flower of Norwegian and Southern womanhood needs food and blankets. It would be unchivalrous, and a bad example, to send Miss Rosemary Elizabeth Lipking back to the Shakers hungry and shivering."

With more whoops and hollers, the highwaymen tumble a pile of cured ham, cheese, apples, and bread loaves at my feet. China and silver cutlery appear as if by magic from saddlebags. A man steps forward and places a waxed wicker picnic basket in the empty traces. Another man folds a geese-on-the-wing quilt into the driver's box.

Their leader roars in laughter as he leaps onto his horse. Her black coat and eyes gleam like obsidian in the moonlight. The huge mare rears up and scrapes the air in front of her. Horse and rider are magnificent, like a painting. He stands upright in his stirrups and doffs his hat with an air that is more mocking than respectful.

"Do you know who I am, Miss Lipking?"

"I reckon I do." *John Hunt Morgan—the king of horse thieves.*

" 'Norwegians are hearty folk,' " he calls out. "You've given me no choice but to believe you. Take care, Miss Rosemary Elizabeth Lipking." The black mare rears up again, but their leader's tone turns serious. "I am sorry about the Shaker sister. Her name was Agnetha? Was she a Southerner?"

I think quickly. "She was left at Pleasant Hill as a child."

"What's her family name? Who's she kin to?"

No one uses family names at Pleasant Hill. "I reckon it was Center—Sister Agnetha of the Center Family."

Their leader hollers, "Men! We ride out!"

A highwayman has already tied Obadiah to another rider's saddle horn. He's nickering to me, his eyes wide and questioning. With more whoops, shouts, hollers, and bursts of rapid gunfire, the Raiders leap onto their horses and gallop after John Hunt Morgan into the night.

They've left Sister Agnetha on the Pike, and me next to the buckboard, without so much as a backward glance.

10

Pleasure

Ma believes in ghosts. She says a ghost wanders among the living after a sudden death, because the soul didn't have enough time to make things right and prepare for its departure. Ghosts don't understand they're dead, Ma says, so they seek out the living for aid, comfort, and consolation.

These days (and especially these nights) there must be thousands of ghosts wandering across hundreds of battle-fields. I stand frozen, afraid to look anywhere, afraid of Sister Agnetha's ghost.

It's a hot night but my flesh is crawling. *What do I do now?*

A freshening breeze picks up. I clamp my elbows to my sides yet start to tremble. It does no good to tell my-self that a breeze, so welcome on a hot afternoon, is terri-fying at night only because the sun is down.

Terror and dread can't be reasoned away.

How quickly the world can change! It can't have been more than five minutes since Sister Agnetha and I were arguing, and now everything is different.

I understand how the ghosts feel.

I won't look at her, lying face up against the front left wheel of the buckboard. I rub my hands against Mr. Hall's wooden box. The hasps twinkle like dew in the moonlight. The smooth box comforts me and makes me think of his daughter, Ellen Hall. Sister Patience could tarry all day in the hayloft of the East Family's cow barn, playing with the kittens. She tames, names, and befriends each one. "Cats are born wild," she says. "It's a cat's true nature to be wild, Sister Bess."

A circle of kittens, each no bigger than a minute, mewl and claw at one another as they snatch chicken scraps and dabs of cream from a plain Shaker plate. Within an afternoon they're tame, accepting pets from each of us, their mother purring and catnapping close by.

Sister Patience, what's your true nature?

Once in a blue moon I've seen the Shaker perfection slip and the person underneath shine through. Sister Patience loves kittens, Eldress Mary loves chocolate cake, Sister Emily drinks extra coffee—that's their true nature. That's why I'm so glad to see it. They're not angels after all.

What's my true nature?

What's Sister Agnetha's? She's terrified of horses. . . .

My flesh crawls again. Out of the corner of my eye I see her stark white clothes like a drift of snow on dark, late-winter ground. She'll have grass stains—an imperfection. We're to take good care of our clothes until they wear out. My heart beats wildly. *Don't look! Don't look!*

I'm miles from Pleasant Hill, without a horse. I can't pull the buckboard! I'm so thirsty. I can't leave Sister Agnetha. In the morning, someone will come along on the Harrodsburg Pike. Someone will pity me and help me. But what do I do now?

The highwaymen left me a feast; my stomach growls as a reminder. I seize a plate, silverware, the loaf of bread, the ham, and the cheese in one quick motion. I eat as though starving. A few minutes later I'm bent over, retching it all up. Half-chewed food splashes against the left front wheel of the buckboard and onto Sister Agnetha.

Sweat rolls down my back as cold chills leave me shaking. My mouth is as stinging-sour as vinegar.

I'll get you home somehow, Sister Agnetha.

Pleasant Hill's graveyard is far to the west of the West Family's dwelling, between the duck pond and the West Lot Family's gristmill. In June, Pleasant Hill's oldest Shaker, Sister Orpah, died. Eldress Mary held the service, and only sisters were allowed to attend.

Shaker markers are pale limestone, hewed right out of the North Family's quarry, yonder by the Kentucky River. Our blacksmith and stonemason, Freeman Thomas Jones, pounds out the inscriptions: SISTER MARGARET, or BROTHER ABRAHAM, and the year of passing.

SISTER AGNETHA 1862. That and a pine box are all she'll get as a remembrance. She'd have thought it was a good reflection on her life—simple, humble, modest, noble, somber, free.

It's strange how thinking about Sister Agnetha's body at rest brings me almost as much comfort as thinking about Sister Patience taming the kittens. *I'll do right by you, Sister Agnetha. I'm very sorry. I will do right by you.*

I stand next to the buckboard for I don't know how long, elbows pressed against my ribs, staring at my feet, trembling. From far down the Pike I hear a sound, a rhythmic squeaking. My heart pounds: a gibbering ghost? No, it's an axle in dire want of grease.

Another carriage is coming up the Harrodsburg Pike. A ghost carriage? Come to collect her? *Don't look at it!* I squeeze my eyelids shut.

"Sister Bess?" a soft voice calls out. "Is that you?"

Brother Daniel! I'd forgotten completely about Brother Daniel. "It was Morgan's Raiders!" I scream. "They stole Obadiah! Sister Agnetha's dead!"

The axle creaks louder as Brother Daniel jumps out of the meadowbrook. He's standing beside me. "Sister Bess! Are you all right?"

"No!" I start to cry and can't stop. Daniel holds me. He doesn't tell me to hush, or stop, or that everything is going to be all right. He lets me cry, just as I let Isaac cry when he wants Ma.

It's a long time before I stop. I step back, away from him.

He says gently, "Sister Bess, we need to put Sister Agnetha in the buckboard. We need to lift her off the ground. Will you help me?"

Horror! "I've never touched a dead person before."

"Nor have I. I'll help you if you help me, and we'll both help Sister Agnetha. Can you do that for her?"

I take a deep breath of humid air, like breathing through a warm dishrag. "Quickly, before I change my mind."

Brother Daniel takes her shoulders and I hoist her feet. In one motion we lift Sister Agnetha and place her, as gently as her weight allows, in the back of the buckboard. This morning's ice has melted, but a hint of cold air remains.

All at once I feel better, because Sister Agnetha would feel better, now that she's off the ground and safe in the buckboard.

Brother Daniel pulls her sunbonnet over her face. Her body glows pure white in the moonlight. I thank God that it's still too dark to see her face.

"Did you say Morgan's Raiders shot her? I don't see any blood."

"They were going to shoot her because she wouldn't give up Obadiah. Could her heart just stop, from fright?"

"I've heard that can happen. Sister Bess, why don't you lie down under yonder tree and sleep? It's a few hours until dawn."

I can't. The tree is too far away. It's too dark.

"I'll sleep on the opposite side after I've tended to Molly," he continues. "Everything will look better when the sun comes up, Sister Bess. I promise."

"Will you walk over there with me?" I feel close to tears again.

"Of course. Here's a quilt from the buckboard."

Despite my fear, I fall asleep like a stone, wrapped in a stolen geese-on-the-wing quilt.

Once again I dream of the Shaker horses in the North Family's pasture. John Hunt Morgan's black mare is among them—she's the queen of the meadow. She gallops, charges, leaps, and kicks while the Shaker horses watch in awe. Soon they join her in the horseplay. Their hooves against the bluegrass sound like distant thunder on a summer's day.

Sister Patience stands at my elbow. Her plain, earnest face, her dreamy blue eyes, are turned toward me. "Unbridled glee," she says, and nods as though I'll understand.

I open my eyes to daylight and Brother Daniel tossing a hatful of water onto the buckboard's left front wheel. "Last night I was so scared, I threw up," I call out sheepishly.

By daylight I feel so foolish—what was there to be scared about? I know the Harrodsburg Pike like the back of my hand. Sister Agnetha's soul surely ascended into Heaven. Her ghost couldn't have been on the Pike last night.

It's Ma's fault I was scared. She filled my head with ghost stories.

While I slept, Brother Daniel took Molly out of harness. She must have grazed for hours. Now she stands over a rippling brook, drinking. Brother Daniel scoops up another hatful of water and pours it on the left front wheel.

I expect him to tease me about retching; any other boy surely would. Instead, he holds a rope up for me to see.

"I found this in the buckboard. I'll tie it to the mead-owbrook, and Molly will have to pull both. You can sit in the meadowbrook if you want. I'll walk and keep a weather eye on the buckboard. And Sister Agnetha."

"I can walk." I don't want him thinking I'm just a silly girl.

Upstream from Molly, I swish my mouth with water as sweet and cold as icehouse butter. All at once I feel shy. "Thank you for packing the food in the wicker basket. Varmints would have eaten everything."

It's well past dawn. The sun is halfway between the horizon and the meridian. It must be nine or ten o'clock. I thought I'd wake at four thirty; that's what I'm used to. Maybe I went to sleep at four thirty?

We walk. After mooning over Brother Daniel for months but not being able to talk to him, now I'm tongue-tied. We walk for more than an hour, I reckon, in deep silence, the Harrodsburg Pike rising gently the whole time.

Brother Daniel smiles at me during quick worship. In June he winked at me, even before Isaac announced to everyone that I was sweet on him. Brother Daniel can't be a Shaker, then; he doesn't believe in the separation. So why is he at Pleasant Hill?

Talking to a young man, being alone with a young man—according to Mother Ann Lee this is the worst, the very worst imperfection of them all. The Shaker path is designed to avoid this very thing. Even non-Shakers wouldn't approve—Ma certainly wouldn't—despite the dire straits we're in.

I take a quick glance at Brother Daniel. He looks the way I feel: tired, fearful, worried, and anxious. Our dire straits are magnified by the Shaker separation, aren't they? We're tired because we slept on open ground. We're fearful because the highwaymen might return. We're worried about Obadiah. We're anxious because of the trouble we'll be in at Pleasant Hill. Worst of all, Sister Agnetha . . .

None of this would have happened, none of it, had we spent the night in the Kettlemans' guest rooms. I think of the good breakfast Mrs. Kettleman would have offered, and my stomach rumbles. Most of our troubles are because of the teachings of Mother Ann Lee.

Ma, families are supposed to live as families. Our family was far from perfect, but it was a family, wasn't it?

At the top of a crest, the blue hills and dales dip and rise in front of us. On the farthest horizon, the hills poke through the clouds like Christmas snow swirled around rocks.

We stop together, as if planned, just for the unexpected pleasure of taking in the view. I speak up. "Do you see how those hills and valleys roll up and pitch down, and each peak is a lighter shade of blue than the one before it? The last one dissolving into sky? Ma says there's a Cherokee word for it—*cataloochee.*"

"*Cataloochee,*" Brother Daniel echoes slowly. "That does sound appropriate. Maybe you'd like to rest and eat something? When did the Kettlemans give you the food?"

"You must be starving! I'm hungry, too. Of course we'll stop."

I spread the picnic cloth and lay out the food while

Brother Daniel unhitches Molly. The mare lowers herself to the ground, rubs her back in the bluegrass, and groans in contentment. Then she hoists herself up and shakes like a dog. The shuddering dust lifts from her back and is borne up by the wind.

I open a pretty gilt mustard pot, and just for pleasure I spread some mustard on a slice of clove-studded ham. I make a sandwich of ham, sharp cheese, and bread. It's delicious. "How wonderful to combine food again! Each complements the other."

Brother Daniel piles ham and cheese onto bread as well. "It's been years since I've eaten a sandwich. This is mighty tasty."

He looks thoughtful for a moment.

"You have a ma?" he asks. "She told you about the *cataloochee?*"

I speak bitterly. "She abandoned us at Pleasant Hill. Last spring Isaac and I used to wait at the front gate for her on sunny afternoons. She isn't coming back—we both know it."

"Abandoned? Surely she'll come back after the war."

"It's the right word. Isaac has changed; he's so cold and far away. Even when I talk about the good times at home—our suppers with Ma, the Godfreys' library, Lucy and her kittens—all he talks about now is perfection on the Shaker path. He looks at Anne and me as though we're bad: His own sisters an imperfection."

"I like Isaac," Daniel says gently. "He talks without end about the cows, the horses, the goats, the sheep. He's named the kittens, and the calves, the lambs, the kids...."

Four of the plow horses will foal next spring. Your brother has names for the foals, too."

"Isaac has always loved baby animals. It makes me sad that he's pulled away from me. I've lost him."

"And you miss your ma," Daniel adds.

"Pa's a drinking man," I say softly. "I've often wondered if Ma thinks Pa needs her more than we do. We're safe; he's Pa."

How wonderful to share my troubles with another.

Finally, I say, "That's the difference, I suppose. An imperfect life is a churning sea of troubles. Shaker perfection has no troubles to speak of."

Brother Daniel smiles. "You haven't lived with the Shakers long enough, Sister Bess. I've lived among them for five years. They're no more perfect than you or I. The difference is, they can't abide knowing it. It fills them with shame. That's why every moment of every day is taken up with toil and prayer. They don't want the time to think."

I ask softly, "So . . . you're not a Shaker?"

Brother Daniel grins. "I'm a winter Shaker. How about you?"

I grin back. "I'm a winter Shaker, too. Y'all have people?"

"I did. Ma and Pa are dead. Typhoid. A neighbor on the other side of the hollow brought me to Pleasant Hill when I was twelve." Abruptly, Brother Daniel stands and walks to Molly. The mare nickers to him, and he speaks softly to her, strokes her nose. His shoulders sag. Their deaths are painful to talk about.

I look away and catch sight of the wooden box Mr.

Hall gave me. I open it and gasp: inside are two pistols with ivory handles, two shot glasses, a silver flask, a leather pouch full of gunpowder, a twist of coarse cotton, and four bullets. Everything is embedded in crushed red velvet.

"Look at this!" I tilt the open box so he can see.

He snorts. "Stolen. All this food, the plates and cutlery, those dueling pistols, everything. Morgan's men will steal anything not nailed down."

"They stole Obadiah, too."

"Obadiah knows his way back to the barn, Sister Bess. He may surprise us."

I smile at him. "You should call me Rosemary Elizabeth. That's my name."

He smiles back. "You should call me Dan."

We sleep for hours after our meal. It's late afternoon before I pack up the plates and silver. I study the wicker basket as if I've never seen a picnic basket before, and that's when I say what's on my mind.

"It's my fault Sister Agnetha died," I say. "If we hadn't been arguing, if I hadn't been singing in my loudest voice to vex her, the Raiders would never have found us. They would never have stolen Obadiah."

Dan shakes his head. "You can't blame yourself for her death, or for a stolen horse. The Raiders heard the singing wheels and the harness jingling. I was on the Pike as well, Rosemary Elizabeth. Why do you think they didn't steal Molly? She's too old and winded. They could tell, just by listening to her plodding hooves, that she's too old for them."

"There's more. Sister Agnetha gave us the task to charm the soldiers—the school sisters, I mean. We charm the soldiers in the food lines so the kitchen sisters can remain separate and perfect. I wanted to show Sister Agnetha how important hospitality is, so we sat there sipping tea in the Sunday parlor even though I *knew* Sister Agnetha wanted to leave. I showed her, didn't I?"

I start to cry again. "Good manners mean nothing in wartime. A silly tea party! And now she's dead."

Once again, Dan waits for me to stop crying. He waits a long time.

"My mother used to invite ladies over for tea," he says. "I used to laugh at the fuss—store-bought tea and lemons from Harrodsburg, three different kinds of tea cakes, and her own briar jam. Before the party Ma and me would have our own tea party. I could eat as many tea cakes as I wanted. She never begrudged me." He wipes his eyes. "If I have to join this war, my mother's tea parties are what I'll think about while marching, maybe even while fighting. Kindness matters. What's the point, if we're not kind to one another?

"The kindest thing we can do now is take Sister Agnetha home."

We hitch up Molly and commence to walk. No one is in the tobacco or cotton fields or sitting on porches in the heat of the day. There is no one on the Harrodsburg Pike. These days the masters are either in the fight or protecting their property. It's the slaves who run errands and deliver messages. But war-torn Kentucky is empty this day.

Whenever we cross a stream, we drink and splash

water on our hot necks and hands. We take turns using Dan's hat to bring water to Molly.

We say nothing to each other, but it's a comfortable silence. I can tell, just by walking alongside him, that Dan is used to keeping his own counsel. How long ago, I wonder, did he part company with the Shakers and yet decide to still live among them? I feel the chafe, and I've only lived at Pleasant Hill for six months.

We're winter Shakers, all right.

We're almost to Pleasant Hill, but we stop by a creek to once again water Molly. Finally, I ask Dan about Sinai's Holy Plain. Does he intend to stay? Or will he leave and join the war? And for which side, Union or Confederate?

Instead of answering, Dan looks down the hollow toward the Kentucky River. In the long summer twilight, the hemlocks, oaks, hickories, beeches, buckeyes, and sycamores glow a rich, glossy green.

"Kentucky hardwoods and Kentucky pine," Dan says after a bit. His voice is low and thoughtful. "There's nothing prettier than the wood grain in a Kentucky hardwood or Kentucky pine." He takes off his hat and wipes his sweaty brow with a sleeve.

"I like Shaker furniture," he continues. "I like it very much. I watched you yesterday, taking in the furniture in the Kettlemans' parlor. It was all so dark, squat, and unyielding, cluttered with curlycues, folderol, false pride, and vanity. I could tell you didn't like it any more than I did."

"I didn't like it. But have you ever noticed? In a Shaker room, you can't tell anything about the people who live there. Isn't that peculiar?"

Dan raises his eyebrows. "You're right. It is singular. The Kettlemans' parlor speaks volumes. Sad thing is, they probably don't know any better. They think their furniture is what furniture is supposed to look like. That's not the Believer way. Shaker furniture is clean, spare, simple, modest, quiet. And useful." Here Dan nods his head for emphasis. His red hair shines. "Everything about it is useful. And it's so light, the grain of the wood shines through. Wood grain is beautiful—it's always different, yet always the same.

"I'm learning to make Shaker furniture in the woodworking shop." He takes a deep breath. "I'd like to stay until I master cabinetry with surety of purpose. Then, after the war, it would be my pleasure to open a furniture shop in a big city—Cincinnati or Pittsburgh, Louisville or Lexington. Maybe even Washington City."

"That's a good plan." I'm thoughtful. "There's something about pleasure; I have yet to reason it out. Each person's pleasure belongs to that person. Aren't we supposed to have our own pleasure? Whatever it is that makes us happy? And if that's so . . . why do the Shakers have no use for it? In their Heaven on Earth, we're all supposed to be the same."

Dan grins at me. "That's exactly right, Rosemary Elizabeth. We're all supposed to be perfect. The Shaker path obliterates all the bad things about human nature: selfishness, laziness, irresponsibility, dishonesty. I do admire that side of it."

I speak up. "I admire it, too. The Shakers work so hard."

"But the Shaker path obliterates all the good things as

well: our talents and enthusiasms, our sense of humor, whatever makes each of us shine in God's eyes. Last winter I made a chest of drawers for the mayor's house in Cincinnati. The beech wood was sent all the way from North Union, near Cleveland.

"I like beech; the wood grain has a pleasing shilly-shally to it. I wanted to use beech for the drawer knobs, too, but no, I couldn't do that. The Kentucky Shakers use *birch* for drawer knobs. Birch wood is so pale; the knobs can be seen in the dimmest of light. Birch is practical." He sighs. "My beautiful beech-wood chest of drawers . . . rendered practical."

"Mother Ann Lee had something to say about drawer knobs?"

Dan grins. "Apparently, Mother Ann Lee had something to say about everything. These are good people, Rosemary Elizabeth; don't misunderstand me. They hate this war as much as they hate slavery. And I agree with them on both counts. Shakers can't abide contradiction, but that's what war is, isn't it? Hate the war but love the purpose."

The sunset warms Dan's face, now peaceful and calm. He's said his piece, I reckon, after five long years of keeping those thoughts inside. I hope he stored them up to share with me.

In the gloaming, the white fences of Pleasant Hill glow like a cloud ring around a hill. I laugh out loud, for there is Obadiah in the North Family's pasture, grazing contentedly in the shade of the North Family's barn.

Obadiah is a smart horse. He knows it's cooler in the shade, and that flies don't see well in it. Bluegrass is particularly tender and succulent when protected by shade. Obadiah not only found his way home, he found the best place in Pleasant Hill to wait and watch for us.

Dan whistles. Obadiah looks up and with a deep whinny breaks into a full gallop. He jumps right over the back pasture fence, his makeshift reins flying behind. He trots over to us. Dan cuts the reins clean off with one of our picnic knives and removes the bridle. Obadiah shakes his head with pleasure.

"You're lucky you didn't trip on those reins, boy," I say.

Obadiah grunts and pushes his forehead against my shoulder in greeting.

I pull some grass and hold it out to him. He eats with relish, even though he's been eating the same all day. I rub between his ears. "Obadiah! What a smart horse you are."

Dan says, "Horses always know the way back to the barn."

Obadiah and Molly press nose to nose and sniff hard. We rub Obadiah's neck while he rubs his forehead against his dam's withers. I tell him again how clever he is.

"Brother Daniel?" A North Family brother stands before us, pitchfork in hand. "You were expected yesterday."

"Brother Noah, we had quite a tangle on the Harrodsburg Pike."

"John Hunt Morgan and his Raiders!" I exclaim. "Sister Agnetha is in the buckboard. She died trying to keep them from stealing Obadiah.

"But you ran away from them, didn't you, Obadiah? You knew the way back to the barn, and you were waiting for us. Good boy!"

As I'm speaking, Brother Noah looks offended, shocked, alarmed, and then offended again. He peers into the buckboard. I see Sister Agnetha just as he sees her: a stout, dead sister with grass stains and retch all over her white Shakeress clothes. Brother Noah never knew her, and now he never will.

"Sister Agnetha was so much more than this. She risked her life; she—"

Brother Noah just looks away. "Brother Daniel, you'll take the sister to Brother Thomas?" he asks. "Freeman Thomas Jones?"

That's meant as a reproach to me. That's four imperfections—sleeping under the same tree with Brother Daniel, walking with him today, talking to Brother Noah, and talking to Obadiah—and I've not yet entered the back gate.

"I'll take Obadiah to his stall," I say. "It must be almost time for supper."

Dan gives me a short nod, but Brother Noah looks offended anyway. His neck stiffens, his eyes glare, his lips crimp together. I've seen that same affronted look on the face of Shaker after Shaker for months now.

The ridiculous separation! Sister Agnetha was terrified of Obadiah, but she gave her life to save him. Because of the separation, Brother Noah will never appreciate what she did for the Pleasant Hill Shakers.

Ridiculous! "Obadiah," I say, as plain as day, "do you

know your way back to your stall?" Obadiah twitches his ears, as though deep in thought. "Good boy."

"I'll take Molly to her stall first," Dan says in Brother Noah's direction. But I can tell from the soft tone in his voice that he's talking to me.

"Obadiah? Do you know 'The Verdant Groves'? That's such a pretty song." I step to the left of Obadiah and curl my right hand around his mane, and with the gentlest of pulls he is walking next to me.

We pass shocked Shakers, each with his or her head poking out of a weaving shed, or a broom shop, or a stable, or a carpenter's shop.

I sing with pleasure, right into Obadiah's left ear:

> "Now we walk in the verdant groves,
> Where lilies fair are growing.
> Here in love and sweet repose
> And gentle rivers flowing."

Obadiah stands in his stall and looks at me expectantly. The other horses are stretching their necks out of their own stalls, nickering and nodding to him.

"Excuse me." My voice is sharp. Two East Family brethren stand openmouthed in the aisle. They're shocked to their foundations, I reckon, to see a school sister in their horse barn.

I'm dead tired, but I give Obadiah water, a pitchfork of hay, and a can of Shaker sweet feed. I clean his hooves and brush his coat as he eats. "Good night, boy," I say, shutting the bottom half of his stall door.

In the Meetinghouse, the Shakers are in the throes of quick worship. I hear them all the way out here on the East Family's side of Pleasant Hill.

Dan and I missed supper. The truth be told, I'm too tired to eat anyway.

There's nothing to be done but walk to the girls' side of the Center Family dwelling. Without taking off my filthy clothes or boots, without kneeling and praying on my angel rug, without folding my arms and arranging myself as an angel, I lie down on my bed, curl into a ball, and sleep.

Later I wake to the soft snores of Sister Jane and Sister Lucy. They must have seen me asleep, wearing yesterday's dirty clothes and two days of dirt and grime on my face and hands. I'm wearing dusty Believer shoes on what was a perfectly clean Shaker bed; it must be filthy.

All in a rush, I'm reminded of my imperfections. I quarreled with Sister Agnetha. I talked to Mr. Kettleman. I've eaten sandwiches, and I've made them from stolen food. I've talked to an animal and expected a reply. I've slept under the same tree as a Shaker brother and talked to him. I've expected a reply and received it. I've sung a perfect Shaker hymn to a horse.

I've deliberately and intentionally walked off the Shaker path.

As I strive toward Shaker perfection, all I think about are my imperfections. All I think about is what I'm doing wrong: waking wrong, dressing wrong, walking wrong, talking wrong, praying wrong, eating wrong, working wrong, sleeping wrong, probably even dreaming wrong.

I'm a bad daughter, an ungrateful resident of Pleasant Hill, and an unloving sister to Isaac and Anne. It's being here again that reminds me of all my imperfections. But if it weren't for Pa, we'd all be home.

We wouldn't have been abandoned and forced through the Shaker sieve.

I understand, suddenly, why the Shakers keep themselves so busy, why every moment of every day is filled up with work.

Life itself is the imperfection.

11

Hearts and Hands

Gong, gong, gong, gong . . . gong.

I dress myself as a Shaker. It feels good to wear clean, fresh-smelling clothes again, but I don't start with my right side. Sisters Jane and Lucy stare at me but say nothing. I wince at the dirt on my hands and the grime under my fingernails. More imperfections.

I wash my hands, face, and neck for a long time.

I grasp a broom and sing the sweeping song, louder than the rest:

> "Sweep, sweep, and cleanse the floor,
> Mother's waiting by the door."

The girls continue to stare as we stand in line for the outhouse.

In the Sisters' Waiting Room the school sisters stare at me in shock. No one even pretends to pray—Sister Agnetha's chair is empty.

After the breakfast broad grace, Eldress Mary stands in the women's doorway of the Center Family dwelling. She shoos me away: "Sister Bess, you have eggs to break." I cross the lane with the gasps and murmurings of school sisters in my ears.

Thank you, Eldress Mary, for telling them about Sister Agnetha's death.

I have two thousand eggs to break, but only after Sister Emily inspects my hands for dirt. She makes me wash them twice more with a potato brush.

After the nooning, and prayers in the Sisters' Waiting Room, I stand by the left side of the yard and call out to passing brethren, "Where's my brother? Where's Isaac Carl Lipking?"

The black-coated brothers turn away. The backs of their necks have that stiff, offended quality. I'm tired of giving offense! I'm tired of such a complicated life! "Where's my brother? Where's Isaac Lipking? Is he with Brother John?"

The brethren walk up the men's stairs of the Center Family dwelling. "Tell Isaac Lipking his sister's here, safe and sound," I call out to them. "I'll wait for him in the front yard of the Trustee's Office, just as always."

I don't have to wait for long. Almost immediately, Isaac runs down the men's staircase. I press him against me and hold him tight. He smells so clean! The familiar scent of daffodil-scented Shaker soap rolls over me like a wave. His clothes smell of lemons and lavender. His ribs feel as delicate as a bird's.

We sit down on the iron bench. "Sister Bess, I thought

you were dead, or run off," Isaac cries. "I thought you'd left me, like Ma!"

"Isaac, I'll never run off, never," I say fiercely. I put my arms around him. "Sister Agnetha died when we tangled with John Hunt Morgan's Raiders. The Raiders let me go. They stole Obadiah, but he came back all on his own. I met Sister Patience's father."

We hold each other for a long time.

"There's another litter of kittens in the East Family's hayloft," Isaac whispers, breaking away from me. "Six of them. They remind me of Lucy's kittens. Do you want to meet them? They don't run off, not from me."

"I'd like nothing more," I whisper back.

In the hayloft, the kittens' squealing mews echo off the walls and stout ceiling beams. Obadiah is out to pasture; there are no horses in the barn.

Kittens tussle in our laps, fighting and biting. They crawl up our forearms and practice pouncing on their siblings. Their eyes gleam fiercely as they bite an ear or clamp their needle-like fangs into another's neck. They squeal and kick. They keen loudly as they tumble in our Shaker clothes.

Isaac has names for them all: Tiger, Dusty, Thistledown, Feathertail, Tomboy. "This one's my favorite. This is Lucy."

Lucy fits into my brother's hand. Lucy the kitten looks just like Lucy the cat, the one we left on Mr. Godfrey's dairy farm: she's black with three white boots. Isaac holds her to his face. "Lucy, you look just like Lucy, don't you?" he asks her. She closes her eyes and sniffs Isaac's eyebrow.

Their mother is nearby, her front paws tucked primly

beneath her, eyes closed. Her purring rises like heat on a summer's day.

Isaac takes a deep breath. "Sister Bess? Mr. Godfrey was here yesterday. Pa's dead."

I catch my breath, too. *Pa's dead?*

"Mr. Godfrey said he put Pa out on the Pike last spring. Pa joined a regiment of Kentucky Confederates. He was killed in the battle of Red Bird Creek. Mr. Godfrey said it was Kentuckian against Kentuckian, brother against brother, and the Confederate Kentuckians lost. They were driven across the Cumberland Gap and into Virginia."

"Was Ma with him? Ma's here?"

"Ma's not here. Mr. Godfrey said she's working in a Union hospital in Lexington."

Relief floods over me. *Ma is a nurse! She's saving soldiers! Maybe the same soldiers I fed.* "She didn't abandon us! She loves us!"

Isaac doesn't look convinced. "Why didn't she tell us she was in Lexington? She could have sent word by Mr. Godfrey. Or a sick soldier could have written a letter for her."

The kittens have settled down and are sleeping contentedly in his lap. He lifts Lucy up and kisses her on her forehead.

"Isaac, as soon as we're able, we'll go to Lexington and find Ma. We can't stay here among the Shakers. Don't you feel it—that relentless Shaker perfection, crushing the life right out of you? Pleasant Hill is like a prison. Why should we remain here if we haven't done anything wrong?"

My brother speaks in a measured, smooth tone. "Pa was an imperfection. But Ma is much worse an imperfection than Pa. Brother John says that by staying with Pa, she put us in harm's way. And she did abandon us. Thank Mother Ann Lee for that—we shouldn't be out among the world's people."

I stare at him in amazement. "We *are* the world's people."

He flinches. "No, we're not! *I'm* not, Sister Bess."

"The only way to learn anything is to make mistakes, Isaac. Lots of mistakes."

Isaac peels a sleepy Tomboy off his shoulder. "My name is Brother Seth. I'm not Isaac anymore."

I gasp. "You're Isaac Carl Lipking!"

"My name is Brother Seth."

I'm so angry, my voice shakes when I speak. "The Shakers won't let you talk to these kittens! Mother Ann Lee said that talking to animals is an imperfection."

Isaac flinches again. He pushes the kittens off his lap. They mew in alarm. Their mother wakes from her catnap and runs to them.

The anger has drained away. "I'm sorry," I say quickly. "I shouldn't have said that. Kittens are *not* an imperfection. Talk to them as much as you want."

Isaac folds his hands in his lap. "I am not the world's people."

Anne is learning to walk. When she sees me at the nursery door, she toddles unsteadily toward me, all in a rush, laughing and clapping her hands. She's dressed head to toe

136

in Shakeress white. The three nursery sisters stoop behind her with their arms outstretched, their faces lit up with alarm, ready to catch her if she falls. "Wizzie! Wizzie!" she cries. *Wizzie* was one of her first words, her way of saying Rosemary Elizabeth.

I scoop her up, breathe in her sweet baby scent. "I've missed you, Anne."

In a crib by the east window, another baby commences to howl.

Two sisters scowl at the third. One of them says, "It's your turn, Sister Teresa."

Sister Teresa runs down the right staircase. I take Anne onto the landing to get away from the baby's howling. It doesn't help much.

Sister Mary follows us. She points her finger at me. "Don't let her walk on the staircase. She'll fall."

"Why would I let my sister walk on the staircase?" I retort. In the nursery, the baby howls louder. "Of course she'd fall."

Why is it that the sourest women are put in charge of children? Just the way Sister Agnetha used to, Sister Mary squares her shoulders and purses her lips. She marches back into the nursery.

"Wizzie, Zack?"

Isaac hasn't seen Anne in weeks. "Isaac will see you tomorrow. I promise, I will bring him tomorrow."

The baby howls and howls.

Soon Sister Hannah comes trudging up the right staircase, her face beet red. For the first time ever, she smiles at me.

I smile back. "This is my sister, Anne."

She doesn't stop walking. "Yonder's my baby. His name is Alexander, named after Alexander Hamilton Stephens." The baby commences a fresh yowl. Sister Hannah rushes into the nursery.

Alexander Hamilton Stephens is vice president of the Confederate States of America. Now I know which way Sister Hannah leans in this war.

Holding Anne's hand, I lead her slowly back into the nursery. Sister Hannah has already settled herself and her son in a rocker. He's stopped wailing.

"That's better, ain't it, Alex? You were a hungry little mite," she croons. I pull a ladder-back chair near them.

Sister Mary scoops up my sister. "Let's go outside and see the ducks, Sister Angelica." Baby Anne holds her chubby arms out to me as Sister Mary stalks out of the nursery. The second sister follows.

I call out to my sister, "Tomorrow." I hope Isaac and I will have a long visit with Anne tomorrow. We'll go outside, where the nursery sisters can't disturb us.

Sister Mary's and Sister Edith's Believer boots stomp down the stairs. Anne's cries of "Wizzie!" echo behind them.

"When did you have your baby?" I ask Sister Hannah.

"Sunday. Only five days ago! It's been a trial, working in the East Family's washhouse and running to the nursery whenever he's hungry."

"Why don't you live in the nursery? When Ma had Anne, she stayed in bed for days afterward."

Sister Hannah studies me. "The nursery sisters aren't

particularly hospitable, are they? Don't they make you feel like you shouldn't be here?"

"I've always felt like an intruder, but they so dote on Anne."

Sister Hannah's face is turned toward her baby. "I swear, I spend most of the day running across Pleasant Hill and up and down the women's staircases. When he cries, one of the sisters fetches me."

"Your baby is beautiful," I say to her.

Sister Hannah beams. "His pa is in the fight. When the war's over, we're going to get married."

"Where's he fighting?"

"Last he wrote, he was marching into Virginia, preparing to fight for General Joe Johnston on the banks of the Chickahominy River. That was in late May. Sister Rachel read the letter to me. But I haven't heard news in more than two months."

Sister Teresa comes into the nursery. She's breathing hard—from trudging up the stairs, I reckon. To my astonishment, she scowls at Sister Hannah and Baby Alex.

She asks, "Where's Sister Angelica?"

"*My sister, Anne,* is with the other nursery sisters," I reply. "They went outside."

"Must be walking round the duck pond." She takes a deep breath. "*Sister Angelica* is powerfully fond of ducks."

Her Believer boots clomp back down the staircase. A scent wafts off her; it's familiar, but I can't quite place it.

Sister Hannah raises her eyebrows.

"They've renamed my sister," I say, "as Shakers are wont to do. They claim she's an angel."

Sister Hannah grins at me. "Do you know why Sister Teresa gasps every time she takes the stairs? She smokes. She hides her pipe in the washhouse and smokes behind the corncrib."

"Of course! She smells like Pa's corncob pipe. I knew I knew that smell. Where does she get her tobacco?"

Hannah shrugs the shoulder that's not holding Alex. "From the brethren?"

"Land o' Goshen, that's an imperfection."

Sister Hannah laughs with me.

It's so peaceful, watching Sister Hannah and her baby.

Ma, Pa's dead. On the way to the nursery, I waited to feel . . . something. I don't feel anything but relief. Do you feel the same way, like a burden's been lifted from your shoulders?

The nursery sisters dote on Anne, true enough, but what if they'd turned their backs on her instead? What would have happened then? The horrible thought chills me to the bone. "Don't the nursery sisters dote on your baby?" I ask Sister Hannah.

"Not that I'm aware. One of them comes to the East Family's washhouse and barks out, 'Sister Hannah?' That means Baby Alex is hungry or needs attending. Then it's off I fly, across the backside of Pleasant Hill."

It's because he's a boy; I'm sure of it. How could they do that to a tiny baby?

"Sister Bess, when you're here visiting your sister, would you hold him? I live far yonder in the West Lot Family dwelling, across Shawnee Run Creek. I work in the East Family's washhouse all day. Babies need to be touched. I don't have the time to hold him or play with him."

"Why aren't you in school with the rest of us girls?"

"The sisters aren't going to let me in the school. We're a bad influence, aren't we, Alex?" Her baby, rosy and redolent of milk and damp diapers, sleeps in her arms.

Sister Hannah's hands are bright red from scrubbing Believers' clothes and bedding all day. Washing clothes in this heat! Washing must be the worst sisters' work. Sister Hannah lives farthest from the Meetinghouse and the dining hall.

The men's and women's clothes have separate clotheslines. How could they be so cruel?

I ask Sister Hannah, "What's your name? Your real name?"

She looks at me in surprise. "Hannah Elizabeth Beals."

"My name is Rosemary Elizabeth Lipking. I'll come up here every day, twice a day, and I'll hold Alex."

"I'd be much obliged."

Four or five times a week, Elder Benjamin gives us the war news just before quick worship begins. I've never seen Sister Hannah in the Meetinghouse. "Your beau was with General Joe Johnston in late May?"

Sister Hannah's serene countenance tells me she knows nothing about the crushing Confederate defeat in Fair Oaks, Virginia, or about General Johnston being badly wounded during the battle. "I hope he comes back here real soon, Hannah Elizabeth Beals. You and Baby Alex don't belong here any more than we do."

141

*

Before supper, the school sisters cluster around me in line at the women's outhouses. They pepper me with questions about my adventure.

Sister Jane asks, "What were the highwaymen like, Sister Bess? The worst sort of men among the worst sort of the world's people, to be sure."

"I'm sure some of them *were* the worst sort."

The girls gasp and crowd around tighter, eager to hear more.

"General Morgan let me go. He was quite the Southern gentleman. And I met your father, Sister Patience."

"You and Brother Daniel in the wilderness," Sister Jane prompts. "After Sister Agnetha was called home."

"Yes."

"You must have talked to him." Sister Jane and the other girls hold their breath. "You were with him all night and a day."

"We talked. His parents had the typhoid. He was brought to Pleasant Hill as a child."

"Brother Daniel looks like an angel," Sister Amy gushes. "He must be perfect."

I snort. "Of course Dan isn't perfect! No one is. But I don't know him well enough to know how he's not perfect."

They let that pass. Sister Jane again: "You call him Dan?"

"He asked me to call him Dan. I asked him to call me Rosemary Elizabeth. That's my name."

As the girls exclaim among themselves, Sister Patience

whispers in my ear. "He's so handsome. Are you sweet on him?"

Instead of answering aloud, I squeeze her hand.

She squeezes mine back. "How is my pa?"

"He's fine. He asked about you, if there was enough food here for the winter. He asked if you were happy at Pleasant Hill."

She smiles. "Ma always said I look like Pa."

On the fourth floor of the Center Family dwelling, school starts again. It didn't occur to me to wonder who would be our teacher. Eldress Mary waits by the blackboard for the six of us school sisters to settle.

As always, her shoulders are squared and her carriage is tall. As brisk as a bird, Eldress Mary gives each one of us a cheerful, no-nonsense look. It's hot up here on the school floor in late August. We school sisters have made fans of folded paper and make good use of them. Eldress Mary ignores the sweat dripping off her chin.

"As you all know, Sister Agnetha has gone to her rightful place in Heaven." She glances at me so quickly I wonder if I'm mistaken.

"'Hands to work, hearts to God'—Mother Ann Lee believed girls should be as educated as boys in order to walk the Shaker path. We have no sister who was as educated as Sister Agnetha.

"Sister Jane: Second Corinthians 6:17: 'Wherefore, step out from among them and be ye separate.'"

Sister Jane's countenance drains of color as she walks to the front of the schoolroom.

"Sister Jane has had five years of schooling, three in Nashville and two at Pleasant Hill. From what I've heard, she reads well and is in firm command of arithmetic. Sister Jane will be your teacher."

Eldress Mary nods to Sister Jane. "I'm certain Sister Agnetha kept meticulous lesson plans. Do you know where she kept her lesson book?"

Without a word, Sister Jane pulls a black ledger from Sister Agnetha's desk. "I believe this is it," she whispers.

"A good teacher must speak up," Eldress Mary says briskly. "No mumbling! I must return to the Trustee's Office. Pleasant Hill's accounts won't balance themselves. Girls," she says, brisker still, "I know you will give Sister Jane the same respect you gave Sister Agnetha."

Sister Jane looks askance at us. We look back at them both, as innocent as pie. "Yes, Eldress Mary," we say as one.

Eldress Mary pulls open the door to the hall, then gives Sister Jane a piercing look. "You will keep an eye on these school sisters, will you not? Lead them on the Shaker path."

"Yes, Eldress Mary." She turns to us. "I hope I will not disappoint."

"Excellent." Eldress Mary closes the door behind her.

We all know what "lead them on the Shaker path" means.

The next day, between school and the broad grace before supper in the Sisters' Waiting Room, Sister Patience whispers in my ear again.

"Can you keep a secret? I want to show you something."

I nod, and she leads me to the third-floor landing of the Center Family dwelling. Flush against the three sides of the landing are chests of deep drawers made to fit precisely against the walls. Late-afternoon sun spills onto the chests; the wood is the color of chocolate. Each drawer must be three feet long and a foot deep. I've walked past these drawers hundreds of times, but I've never seen anyone open them.

Sister Patience opens the bottom left drawer on the farthest left side of the wall. "Left and left again," she whispers. "The sisters never open this drawer."

She pulls a white cotton blanket off the top. Deep in the drawer are small parcels wrapped in newspapers.

"This one is mine." Sister Patience unfolds a parcel and shakes out a dark red dress with white daisies embroidered on the hem. She holds the dress to her nose and takes a deep sniff. "When I leave Pleasant Hill," she whispers, "when Pa comes for me, I'm going to walk out of the gate wearing this dress."

She shuts her eyes and sniffs again.

Even I can tell this dress is much too small for her. "How long have you lived at Pleasant Hill?"

"Going on three years. The cloth was from a dress of Ma's. She made me this dress. She embroidered the daisies on the hem. It smells just like her."

"Are my clothes in this drawer?"

"Shh! Of course." Sister Patience pulls out a parcel deep in the bottom of the drawer. She gives me a bundle

145

folded neatly in an old newspaper. It crinkles softly. Inside are the clothes I wore when I first came to Pleasant Hill: the blue blouse and brown skirt, hand-me-downs from Ma; the striped shawl, a hand-me-down from Mrs. Godfrey. I'd thought my clothes had long since been burned.

Sister Patience whispers again. "Smell."

I hold my blouse to my nose and breathe in. Tangy smoke, salt-cured ham, harsh kerosene, the daisy scent of Castile soap, the pungent smell of cheese, and the sweet stink of cow manure—my blouse smells like our cabin, like Ma, and like the cheese and cowsheds of Mr. Godfrey's dairy farm.

My clothes smell of home. To my surprise, my eyes flood. "I'm so homesick," I whisper.

Sister Patience leans forward and whispers, softer still. "We had to be sure we could trust you, Rosemary Elizabeth. Any time the sisters' hands are to work, you can open this drawer and smell your clothes, for comfort. All us school sisters know about this drawer."

I whisper back, "Sister Jane won't mind?"

Sister Patience leans toward my right ear. She smells of chalk, apples, lemonade, and lavender. She smells of Pleasant Hill. "It was Sister Jane who told me to show you the drawer. We have all agreed not to cross her. Eldress Mary won't appoint another teacher if we don't cross Sister Jane."

Sister Patience's blue eyes are dreamy yet solemn. She holds up her right hand, palm toward me. "Because of you, there are kittens at Pleasant Hill. That's why Sister Jane thinks we can trust you with the drawer. Swear."

"Sister Jane isn't one of them?"

"Not at all. She agrees we shouldn't cross her. Swear."

I touch my right palm to hers. "I swear not to cross Sister Jane. I swear to keep this drawer a secret." Sister Patience nods and pulls her hand away.

"Ellen Hall, I forgot! Your father sent you a present— a set of dueling pistols in a polished wooden box, of all things." I grin at her. "Dan must have them."

She grins back. "They're from Pa, and that's what matters."

Sister Patience folds her red dress and places it carefully in the newspaper. She tucks the bundle back into the drawer. She whispers, "Thank you for calling me by my name.... Rosemary Elizabeth, smell all you like, and then fold your clothes away in the newspaper. The newspapers keep the home scents from mixing. They don't suspect a thing, the sisters."

"I'll ask Dan for the pistols."

"Sister Jane walks the Shaker path, but she doesn't expect anyone else to follow her. Kindness is her true nature. "

I reply, "She is kind even as she strives to be perfect."

Kindness, perfection, a true nature, Isaac, Ellen, and Jane . . .

I give my heart to God. Prayers in the Sisters' Waiting Room at broad grace before breakfast, and after breakfast; more prayers in the Sisters' Waiting Room at broad grace before the nooning, and after the nooning; more prayers in the Sisters' Waiting Room at broad grace before supper, and after supper; quick worship, prayer on my angel rug, and then sleep.

I give my hands to work: sweeping, cooking, breaking eggs, peeling apples, making lemonade, and attending school.

It's in the busiest moments of the day, as far away from God as is possible, that I think my deepest thoughts:

Ma, no matter what happens, I have to believe that having Pa gone is a blessing. That's my true nature, Ma—a piece of it, anyway. Pa gone is a relief, like stepping into the icehouse on a hot summer's day.

I will take Isaac to visit Anne, even if I have to drag him up the women's staircase.

I lie awake after bedtime and think about my true nature. How do I know I've found it? Or if what I've found is worth keeping? How will I know? Wouldn't it be easier to be what someone else thinks my true nature ought to be? Why should finding my own path be this hard?

I know this much. Even if I never find it, the search is a blessing, too.

12

Iste Perfecit Opus

I'm to learn broomcraft.

Broomsquires use wood from the sugar maple tree for the handles because the wood is strong and grows straight as an arrow. Broomcorn grows from May to August, and the stalks have been drying in the tobacco sheds for a month. Broomcorn isn't really corn, but the plant is so tall, and the roots are so shallow, that it grows best with cornstalks around it as protection against the wind.

Sister Miriam is our broomsquire. She says that the broomcorn plant comes from Africa and that Benjamin Franklin imported it through Philadelphia as a cash crop. Among the world's people, it's the old salts—retired sailors—who craft brooms, using their sail-making needles and awls. At Pleasant Hill, the job falls to men and women.

The women's broom shop is just behind the brethren's wood shop, on the East Family's side of Pleasant Hill.

While stalks of broomcorn soak in a trough, Sister Miriam teaches me about broom making.

"As Mother Ann Lee has said, 'Good spirits can't live where there is dirt.' Holes have been drilled into both ends of the sugar maple handle. The top hole is for a leather loop: Brooms are much too valuable to leave on the floor, Sister Bess. When not in use, they should be hung on pegs on the wall. There are three holes on the bottom of the handle, three inches apart, for three layers of broomcorn."

She holds up a spool of beige twine. "Jute is a tough string that comes from the Kentucky hemp plant. Loop the jute through the first hole and tie one end tightly. Then wind the other end around a thick oak plank about ten inches long. Tuck each stalk of broomcorn under the jute, put both feet on the oak plank, and pull up to tighten. Wind and pull, wind and pull, until one layer of broomcorn is wrapped all around the handle. Wrap the jute three times around.

"We Believers always nail the wrapped jute securely to the handle. It's what makes our brooms the best. Next, thread the jute through the second hole and tie one end. Wrap a second layer of broomcorn around the handle, pulling and tightening the jute all around. Wrap the jute three times around; nail it tight.

"Now loop the jute through the third hole and tie one end. Wrap a third layer of broomcorn around the handle, pulling and tightening the jute all around. Be sure you've got an odd number of stalks around the third layer for the weave. Wrap it and nail it once more."

My head is swimming. It's back to eggs and apples, I reckon. I'll never learn to how make brooms.

Sister Miriam talks on. "Use the basket weave to weave the jute around the broomcorn stalks that are still above the nailed wraps: over and under, over and under. Here's the reason for the odd number of stalks: We weave thirteen times, to mark the thirteen at the Last Supper. That's called the puritan weave. Trim the broomcorn stalks round the edge of the last weave.

"Now put the broom in a broom vise. Stitch more jute to the broomcorn to form a fan. Cut the broomcorn in a straight line, slightly beveling the edges. And that's all there is to it."

Sister Miriam's black eyes look at me sharply. "I'll be in the weavers' shop if you need me." She returns to the broom shop every few minutes to make sure I haven't committed any imperfections.

After making fifty brooms, five brooms a day, my arms are muscled and my skin is broken, red, and prickly from the "broomcorn itch."

Just behind the brethren's wood shop, I find a hickory stick. It's crooked and almost three times as long as a regular broom handle. Someone has peeled all the bark off it. I like the dips and whorls in the hickory wood; sugar maple wood has almost no grain.

I turn the hickory stick into a broom handle: loop three times, nail, loop three times, nail, loop three times, nail, weave, stitch, vise, and trim. I could craft brooms in my sleep.

The broom shed has its own ladder. I hang the hickory-wood broom from the uppermost peg on the broom wall. Unlike all the others, its handle is crooked, not straight.

Sister Miriam points. "That broom is twice an imperfection," she snaps. "The handle is crooked, and it's much too long."

I knew she'd say so, and I'm prepared. "No, no, it's just right. Isn't the hickory pretty? I *like* the bend in the handle. It's perfect. It's mine."

Sister Miriam looks startled, then vexed. She says nothing more as she settles next to her vat of soaking broomcorn.

It's mine. I haul the hickory-handle broom and the ladder up the right staircase to the Children's Order of the Center Family dwelling. With my *left* Believer boot, I pound a nail directly above my bed, just below where the wall meets the ceiling, and hang my broom high. I stand by my bedfoot to admire it. It looks so pretty against the butter-yellow walls: The jute twine woven tightly around the broomcorn stalks looks like a Shaker basket.

Sister Amy asks me if my broom is for the morning sweeping of the floor.

"No," I say quietly. "It's for looking—for the pleasure of looking at it."

Sister Amy looks baffled, but Sister Patience smiles at me.

With a sureness of purpose that is new to me, I take to walking along the banks of the Kentucky River and in the woods around Pleasant Hill, looking for branch and tree fall. I find five likely branches on the forest floor: two of oak, two of sycamore, and the real prize: a branch of mountain ash. Each is about five feet long, and about as big around as Isaac's wrist.

After stripping the branches of bark, I take them to the wood shop. Brethren scatter like frightened birds. "Brother Daniel," I say with a smile, "would you sandpaper these branches smooth for me?"

"I surely will, Sister Bess," he says, smiling back.

"I prefer Rosemary Elizabeth," I say softly. This is the first time we've spoken since the Raiders.

"So do I," he responds, softer still.

Two days later Dan is standing in front of the women's broom shop with the branches. He has sandpapered them all smooth as bone and applied a light furniture oil to make the wood grain stand out. "These are beautiful," I say. "Thank you."

Dan glows with pleasure. "Yes, they are," he says, looking straight at me.

Sister Miriam has her back turned. I give Dan a big smile.

I soak multicolored broomcorn in the broom shed trough and think carefully about which color would look best with each handle. The broomcorn is every hue of cream, honey yellow, light brown, burnt orange, deep brown, mahogany, dark blue, true red, and a sort of reddish purple that's the very color of cranberries.

The soaking broomcorn looks so pretty in the morning sunshine, like a covey of girls whispering

153

secrets, their shiny-clean hair lifting in a sunny breeze.

What with school, daily prayers, visiting with Isaac and Anne and Alex, Obadiah and the barn kittens, quick worship, and my daily five brooms, it takes a week to make my special brooms.

Broomcraft makes me glow with pleasure.

Sister Miriam pretends not to notice, but I catch her looking at my barn brooms.

"I don't think I can bear to sell these, Sister Miriam," I say. "Look at this one, how the mulberry, honey brown, and butter yellow broomcorn are the perfect accompaniment to the mountain-ash handle. See how the same colors are in the handle as in the broomcorn? And how the dark brown jute between the handle and the broomcorn catches the eye first?"

This isn't just a broom. It's something else.

Sister Miriam frowns, but I can tell she admires the mountain-ash broom, for she says nothing to disparage it.

The insides of my arms are red and broken from the broomcorn itch. As I scratch, Sister Miriam frowns. "Leave the itch alone. Scratching makes it worse."

"Sometimes I can't sleep at night, my arms itch so."

"Scratching is the imperfection. Ignoring it is the Shaker path." She holds up her arms. The undersides are red and shiny, as though badly burned.

"How can you stand it?" I ask. "Don't your arms itch all the time?"

"Daily I pray to Mother Ann Lee for deliverance."

I say, "What about Shaker herbs and remedies? There must be something to relieve the itch."

154

Sister Miriam looks thunderstruck. "I hadn't thought of it. I'll go to the women's side of the hospital and ask."

My brooms satisfy me in a way that nothing else does. They're perfect: *my perfect*, I think in shock. My path.

Dan gives me nails and a hammer. I climb the ladder again, pound nails into the apex of the broom shed, and hang my brooms high. They are especially pretty around four o'clock these days, when the sun shines on them.

That no one else in Pleasant Hill seems to admire my brooms the way I do makes the pleasure even greater, if that makes any sense.

That evening my hickory-handle broom, the one I hung above my bed, is gone, as is the nail. The humid air has already closed the nail hole in the wood. There is nothing left to suggest my broom was there at all.

I cry, "How could a Shaker steal my broom?"

Sister Jane touches my elbow. "Eldress Mary would like to speak to you after tomorrow morning's broad grace. She'll wait for you in the Elders' Dining Room. She said you'd know it."

"Is it about my broom?" *Did Eldress Mary take my broom?*

Sister Patience says, "Just before supper she came into our retiring room with a ladder and said something in another language. It sounded like 'perfect,' but she was frowning. She climbed up, pulled the nail out, and took your broom and the ladder with her."

In bed I toss and turn. Hanging my broom above my bed brought me so much pleasure! *An imperfection.* Will

I be breaking eggs again? I haven't yet had to wash clothes and bed linens—will Eldress Mary send me to the laundry?

After broad grace I wait for Eldress Mary. I haven't been in the Elders' Dining Room since my first morning at Pleasant Hill. A vase of peach-colored roses, set perfectly in the middle of the table, fills the room with fragrance.

I don't have long to wait.

"Come with me, Sister Bess." Eldress Mary leads me up the right staircase to the third floor of the Trustee's Office. Her office, a room on the right side, is spacious, with generous windows looking out toward the Meetinghouse. A large desk, bookshelves, and cabinets line the walls. Like everything Shaker made, the furniture is finely crafted. Maple, I'm guessing.

I've seen Mr. Godfrey's office: a welter of papers and ledgers stacked to the ceiling, with pipes, spoons, plates, coffee cups, and teacups scattered on every surface. Eldress Mary's office is spotless; not even one piece of paper is askew. Her bookshelves are full, stuffed neatly to the ceiling with books.

I haven't seen a book in seven months—what would I give for a chance to look through her library? I'd break a million eggs.

She points to a ladder-back chair in front of her desk. I sit down.

Eldress Mary looks me straight in the eye. "Sister Bess, why did you hang that hickory-handle broom above your bed?"

"You don't like it?" I stammer.

"On the contrary; it's exquisite—"

I lean forward. "So you *do* like it?"

She arches her eyebrows.

"I'm sorry I interrupted you, Eldress Mary."

"Forgiven. Sister Miriam has told me you're a hard worker and quite enthusiastic. As an affirmation of Pleasant Hill, you've given the Believers a bright future as a broomsquire."

She looks at me, more keenly still. "Why did you hang it above your bed?"

I squirm. "Because I like it. Because I made it."

Eldress Mary nods. "'Because I made it.'"

I say nothing.

"*Iste perfecit opus.* You don't know what that means."

"No, ma'am."

"That's all right. Live and learn. It's Latin: 'This man made the work.' In the fifteenth century, a monk called Fra Lippo Lippi learned to paint. He'd been orphaned and had lived within a Carmelite order of monks since he was eight years old. They gave him everything he had. Do you understand, Sister Bess? They gave him everything he had."

I nod. *The Shakers have given me food, shelter, and clothing. That's a lot, but that's all.*

"Have you heard of the Renaissance? That's not important. Fra Lippo Lippi painted a masterpiece called *The Coronation of the Virgin* and painted *himself* into the painting. More than that, he wrote '*iste perfecit opus*' in a scroll next to his portrait's praying hands so all would know that *he* had created that painting."

"Yes, ma'am." I shift nervously in my chair.

"You don't perceive the borrowing. Fra Lippo Lippi painted for the glory of himself, and not for the glory of God. That was the Renaissance for you—a celebration of man's self-image. We Believers create everything for the glory of God and Mother Ann Lee. Do you understand?"

"I understand I won't get my broom back," I say sadly.

Eldress Mary looks at me steadily. "I've given your broom to the East Family for their dairy barns. Manure attracts flies, flies attract spiders, and spiders spin webs.

"Your broom is perfect, Sister Bess. It is beautiful, a work of art. Hence it is perfect for sweeping cobwebs from the windows of the East Family's cow barns."

"Yes, Eldress Mary."

"You may go." Eldress Mary reaches for a ledger cornered perfectly on the outside edge of her desk.

My gaze is on her books. I take a deep breath for courage. "How do you know so much?" I ask. "You know about accounting and figures, and the Bible, and art. You must read a lot."

Eldress Mary smiles. "Do you like to read, Sister Bess?"

"I . . . I like to read very much."

"Excellent! 'Hands to work, hearts to God.' It takes two hands to hold a book, does it not? If you'd like to borrow any of my books, all you need do is ask."

"Thank you so much!"

"Again, excellent! You could be one of Pleasant Hill's schoolteachers someday. Sisters Miriam, Emily, and Agnetha have all told me you have a good head on your shoulders. I've been keeping my eye on you, Sister Bess."

I say in my politest voice, "I don't know what I want

to do with the life God has given me, but . . . I can't stay here, Eldress Mary. I reckon I'm just too independent. I'd like to read your books, though, if that's all right."

A quick glance at Eldress Mary shows me her disappointment. She's smiling, but the light has gone out of her eyes. How hard it must be to add to their numbers, for who would want to live such a constrained and hampered life?

"I see. That singularly American independent spirit has given this nation many blessings. You intend to paint yourself into every painting? The constant, deliberate celebration of oneself is hardly a blessing."

"No, ma'am. Fra Lippo Lippi didn't paint himself into every one of his paintings, did he?"

Eldress Mary gives me a startled look. "No, he did not." Briskly, she stands up, reaches to a top shelf, and pulls down a thick black book. "You may start with this: *Italian Renaissance Painters.* Have you been to Florence?"

"Yes, ma'am. Just south of the Ohio."

She says kindly, "That's Florence, Kentucky, dear. My father took me to Florence, Italy, when I was a girl. Travel abroad was called the grand tour in those days. We saw some of Fra Lippo Lippi's paintings there. You may borrow this book; I know you'll take care of it. His paintings, including his *iste perfecit opus,* are in the middle.

"When you've finished, you are welcome to share your ideas with me. The sisters are right—you do have a good head on your shoulders."

I take the heavy book in my hands.

"'Hands to work, hearts to God.' You have work, Sister Bess?"

"Yes, thank you." *Ma would be pleased by your compliments.*

Eldress Mary is already working as I take my leave.

One evening in late August, just before quick worship, Elder Benjamin talked to the brethren's side of the Meetinghouse about the Quaker tradition of referring to the months and days as numbers. The Quakers abandoned the custom of the world's people of naming the months and days for pagan gods and just-as-pagan Roman emperors. Shakers started as Quakers, he reminded the brethren.

The sisters listened, too, of course. Elder Benjamin glanced toward Eldress Mary, who turned to Sister Emily and gave her an enthusiastic nod. Sister Emily nodded in return.

So that's how they do it! I thought. *Communication between the sexes.*

With Eldress Mary's encouragement, Elder Benjamin spoke louder. "I am especially offended by the name the world's people give this month," he said. "Luke 2:1: 'And it came to pass in those days, that there went out a decree from Caesar Augustus, that all the world should be taxed.'

"I'm offended that the United Society of Believers in Christ's Second Appearing should call this month by the name of the very Caesar who taxed the holy family, forcing them to sojourn to Bethlehem. I decree"—here Elder Benjamin sputtered a bit—"I—I *suggest* that this month be known as Eighth Month. Today is Sixth Day, the twenty-second day of the Eighth Month."

There was a murmur of agreement. I sighed: Friday,

160

the twenty-second of August, had become yet another imperfection.

Like a murder of crows bolting off a telegraph wire, the brethren leapt out of their chairs. They landed heavily on the floor. Sisters twirled out of their seats like whirlwinds and began to shriek. Another quick worship had begun.

It's after the nooning, and I'm sitting in front of the Trustee's Office with Isaac. "The twenty-eighth day, First Day of the Ninth Month," he whispers to himself. He frowns in concentration. "No. It's First Day, Ninth Month, the twenty-eighth day. . . ."

"I thought we'd see Anne today." It's Sunday, and the Shakers always take the afternoon to rest. "She asks about you all the time."

"I can't be in the same room as the nursery sisters," my brother says shortly. "*First* Day, twenty-eighth day, Ninth Month . . ."

"I'll take Anne to the duck pond. You needn't set your eyes on the nursery sisters. She's always so happy to see her big brother. She loves you, Isaac. Isn't it amazing? She has no memory of living in a family, but she knows you are her brother."

"Ninth month, First Day, twenty-eighth day . . ."

"No matter how you say it, it sounds silly. It's Sunday, September twenty-eighth. January first marked the first day of the first month of the Roman calendar, so you're back in pagan Rome, anyway."

Isaac looks stricken. "How do you know that?"

161

"I read about it in a book."

"Does Elder Benjamin know that?"

"It'll come to him eventually. . . . Look what I've brought you." I'm holding a trim Shaker basket.

This is my last chance to reclaim you, Isaac. I've been praying at broad grace that this will work.

I tip open the top and a passel of kittens tumble out. Some of them are squealing, kicking, and biting ears. Some are blinking, drowsy in the sunshine.

Within the basket, Lucy the kitten is curled up, fast asleep, the size of a pippin apple. She's adorable.

"She misses you, Isaac." I reach into the basket and take black-and-white Lucy out. She's still asleep and as limp as a damp rag.

"Look," I say. I lift Lucy toward him. "Three white boots. And look." I hold the left back foot toward his face. "A black boot. Three white boots and a black boot on her left back foot. Lucy the kitten looks exactly like Lucy the cat from Mr. Godfrey's dairy farm. I'm sure Mr. Godfrey is taking good care of her.

"I know how much you miss Ma. I know how much you miss Lucy the cat. If you can be strong, if you can hold in your mind all the good things about Mr. Godfrey's dairy farm, if you can look to the front gate and know Ma will fetch us after the war is over, that means we can stay at Pleasant Hill. We can stay here, safe, and still be Isaac, Anne, and Rosemary Elizabeth. We can keep our family."

Isaac is looking at Lucy with tears in his eyes.

"You don't have to talk to her," I say softly. "I know how much you miss Ma and Lucy."

With his left index finger, Isaac strokes Lucy's delicate cheekbones, her tiny chin. She purrs.

To please Sister Jane and Eldress Mary, I walk on the Shaker path. At least my body does. I dress the right side of me first. I sing the sweeping song before dawn. I eat silently and Shaker my plate. I make brooms with handles as straight as arrows. I talk to Isaac only after the nooning broad grace. I start walking with my right foot in all ways. I don't mix food. I work hard. I never complain about anything. But . . . in my mind, I run in the field with the horses.

I hold Baby Alex and rock him to sleep. On hot evenings, instead of quick worship I go to the East Family's barns with apple peelings and carrot knobs from the kitchen for Obadiah and the other horses. Sometimes Ellen Hall and Hannah Beals come with me. We talk to the horses and the cats, kittens, goats, and sheep. I know they listen.

Sister Jane suggests gently that we attend quick worship from time to time, so as not to arouse suspicion.

My hickory-handled barn broom hangs on the wall in the cow barn. It has bits of cobweb on it, so I know the brethren in the East Family are using it to good purpose.

This afternoon there's an apothecary jar of Shaker calamine lotion on my bed. It's wondrously soothing on my inner arms and wrists, the perfect remedy for broom-corn itch. Now I'm sure Sister Miriam approves of my broom making.

Tonight is showery and cool, so I attend quick worship. The Shakers dance all their favorite dances: the

Wheel Dance, the Endless Chain, the Corners of Life, the Angel in the Square. Dan lifts his eyebrows when he sees me.

I dance by him and take a deep sniff. He smells of wood chips, varnish, and paint, from the brethren's wood shop. Once Dan is satisfied that he's mastered the trade, and once this cruel war is over, he'll seek his own fortune. Perhaps I will go with him.

The important thing is that Isaac, Anne, and I will leave Pleasant Hill. The dream of our leaving sustains me. I'm responsible for them now. I know what's best. The relentless Shaker perfection crushes the soul. It squeezes out whatever it is we don't like, but also—especially—what we do like, about ourselves. The Shaker path's costs are too great. I owe my brother and sister a chance to discover their own imperfections.

I dance by Dan again, and he winks. I nod back. The Wheel Dance will go on and on and on. We'll dance by each other all evening.

Elder Benjamin gives the brethren the war news before supper.

"In the Ninth Month, Second Day, the twenty-second day," he begins. Frowning Shakers count on their fingers: Monday, September 22. "President Lincoln issued the Preliminary Emancipation Proclamation. It applies only to those slaves held in territory deemed to be in rebellion and thus out of the Union's hands. Those slaves held in states loyal to the Union—Delaware, Maryland, Kentucky, and Missouri—are not free."

The Shakers groan.

Elder Benjamin raises his hands. "It's all right. It's all right. This really means no slaves are free, but it's a start. Mother Ann Lee was a fiery abolitionist, and the Believers have been so since the very beginning in Niskayuna, in the British colony of New York. There are freemen and freewomen in every Believer village. Mother Lee would be proud of President Lincoln."

The rest of the war news is right here, in the middle of Kentucky. General Bragg's Confederates are trying to push the Union forces north and across the Ohio River. The Union forces are standing fast and don't give an inch.

On October 8, Elder Benjamin reports official word about Morgan's Raiders. They're in Perryville, just ten miles south of Harrodsburg, fighting alongside General Bragg and his men.

The Union forces chase General Bragg's men into retreat, south-southwest toward the Mammoth Cave and into western Tennessee. I wonder if the Raiders have gone into Tennessee as well.

On October 9, there's more fighting near Harrodsburg. That's less than ten miles away. I hear the cannon fire echo off the hills and smell the harsh smell of gunsmoke as the warm afternoon breezes drift toward Pleasant Hill.

We feed no soldiers, and none bed down in the orchards. More Rebels retreat south with the Union in hot pursuit.

The war has finally come to Pleasant Hill.

13

The Ducks

I've been dreading a visit to the cemetery.

The Shaker burial ground is just about the farthest west anyone can go and still remain at Pleasant Hill. Most of Sinai's Holy Plain can be seen from the cemetery, which is on a rise. A Kentucky Shaker knows he or she will have a well-earned rest with Pleasant Hill forever in view.

The headstones are made of Kentucky limestone. The older ones are weathered to anonymity; over time, water dissolves limestone. Shakers long buried here would like that, I reckon, and consider it proper, humble, fitting, and free.

Freeman Thomas Jones's newest headstone reads clear:

SISTER AGNETHA 1862

For the first time, I kneel by the stone. "I'm sorry, so sorry about what happened. I understand now that all you wanted was to lead me on the Shaker path. Believers work so hard to help one another. I think about this war and how quickly it would end if we all worked as hard to help one another.

"You were terrified of horses, but you stood up to the worst of the world's men for Obadiah's sake. I admire you for that. You won't understand this, but when Brother Noah looked at your body with such . . . distance—as though all he could think about was the fact that you weren't a man—I knew I was done with the Shakers."

I brush some dirt from her headstone. "There's been a lot of talk lately about freedom. That's what people say this war is all about. It seems to me that freedom means choosing your own path. You chose yours. I don't know what my path is yet, but shouldn't I be the one to choose it?"

I lift my head and take in all of Pleasant Hill.

The tops of the hardwood trees are fiery plum, red, orange, and yellow. The October sky sparkles clear. The air is cool and dry.

There's the West Family's corncrib, where the runaways hide. There's the Center Family pasture, orchards, water house, and school grounds; the Meetinghouse, the Trustee's Office; the East Family barns, gardens, and greenhouse; the North Family mill wheel and coal fires. Simply and graciously, each makes room for the one after. And all the smaller buildings and sheds seem to have sprung up like mushrooms.

The sound of Shaker work is everywhere: sawing, hammering, chopping, smithing, hoeing, threshing, mixing, stirring, weaving, and hauling. On the men's and women's clotheslines, plain and simple Shaker garments flap tirelessly in the breeze.

"Pleasant Hill is peaceful and serene. Beautiful, even. But angels don't live here. People live here, Sister Agnetha, and doesn't God know that and admire it?"

My sister's clear laughter rings out over the cemetery.

At the edge of the duck pond, the nursery sisters are holding tightly to Anne's hands. Mother ducks have waddled into the water, and their young are jumping, jumping like grasshoppers, into the pond to join them.

These are no longer fluffy, piping ducklings. They stand tall and ruffle their slender bodies to shake the water off their oily, shiny feathers. The young ducks follow behind their mothers as they have done since they were born.

Still laughing, Anne strains against the nursery sisters as they hold her back. Her feet in spotless white boots step forward, and forward again.

I say, "Let go of her hands. She wants to see the ducks." I jump up, wave my arms, and run toward the duck pond. "Let go of her hands! She wants to see the ducks! Let her go!"

The nursery sisters look up, frown at me. At that moment of distraction, Anne breaks free. She toddles toward the duck families.

Ma, Anne is walking outdoors. If only you could see it!

The flock takes off as one, flapping their wings, quacking their complaints.

"Take care," I whisper. The ducks wheel south, toward the worst of the war.

Open-armed, Anne runs after them, her feet splashing muddy water in all directions. As she jumps into the duck pond, her laughter peals outward like a church bell.

Afterword

THE SHAKERS

In early August 1774, Mother Ann Lee and a small band of Shaking Quakers landed on the island of Manhattan, in the British colony of New York. They had been driven out of Great Britain and were hoping to worship freely in the New World. In 1780, they founded the first Shaker village in Niskayuna, near Albany, New York.

The Shakers, officially named the United Society of Believers in Christ's Second Appearing, became an exclusively American denomination. They left no followers in Great Britain.

The Shakers believe in a dual God: Father and Mother. They believe in the three Cs: communal living, celibacy, and, for final-stage Shakers, confession. Their numbers grow only through their missionary work.

There were once twenty-five Shaker communities, mostly in New England and New York, Ohio, and Kentucky. The last Shaker-towns to be settled were White Oak in Georgia, which lasted only from 1898 to 1902, and Narcoossee in Florida (1895-1924).

In the late 1850s, just prior to the American Civil War, the Shakers reached their peak in population and influence. There were eight thousand Shakers living in twenty-two Shakertowns, including Pleasant Hill, Kentucky.

It was the Shakers who started the seed-and-plant catalog business. Shaker seeds became a staple of American farms. The flat broom, another Shaker innovation, has become the standard for the modern broom. The Shakers also invented the circular saw and the clothespin.

The Shakers did not avoid modernity. The Shaker village in Canterbury, New Hampshire, was one of the first places in that state with electricity. Shaker communities owned cars and tractors. The last two Shaker sisters to live in the Shaker village in Canterbury had favorite television shows, including *Wall Street Week* and *The Tonight Show*.

The Shaker village of Pleasant Hill, in Mercer County, Kentucky, was once a community of more than 250 buildings spread out over nearly 5,000 acres. It was founded in 1805. There were five families, each with fifty to one hundred members. The last Shaker there died in 1923.

Pleasant Hill is now a living history museum and is open to the public.

The Shakers were both creative and innovative, and yet everything they made followed inexorably the Shaker path. It is as though one person made everything. I find that astonishing, and my wondering how it could have happened was the impetus for this novel.

In the modern era, Shaker-design furniture, with its clean, simple lines, has become the hallmark of the "country look" in American decor. High-quality furniture and handicrafts are perhaps the Shakers' most lasting legacy.

As of this writing, there are five Shakers left. The sisters are all in their nineties and live in the last active Shakertown, called Chosen Land, in Sabbathday Lake, Maine.

MORGAN'S RAIDERS

John Hunt Morgan was from an old Kentucky family prominent in Lexington society. General Morgan led two major campaigns, one in Kentucky in the summer of 1862, the other in Indiana and Ohio in the summer of 1863. The Raiders rode as far north as Lisbon, in northeast Ohio, the farthest northern reach of the Confederate war effort.

On October 11, 1862, two hundred Morgan Raiders descended upon Pleasant Hill, Kentucky, bent on stealing horses, food, and clothes. The Shakers fed them a breakfast of Shaker ham, eggs, pickled-fruit compote, and Shaker molasses brown bread. Their horses grazed in Pleasant Hill's green pastures while the Raiders slept in the peach orchard.

For dinner the Shakers served the Raiders haunches of roast

venison, mashed turnips and potatoes, more molasses brown bread, and lemonade, with Ohio lemon pie and pudding-in-haste for dessert.

The Raiders stole nothing from the Shakers.

General Morgan was apprehended near East Liverpool, Ohio, in July 1863. With express orders from President Lincoln, he was sent to the Ohio State Penitentiary in Columbus. He escaped, some historians think with help from prison guards, in November 1863.

The self-proclaimed general was caught by Union troops in Lebanon, Tennessee, and shot on sight on September 4, 1864.

Without their charismatic leader, the Raiders disbanded quickly.

Sources

My research for this book included personal visits to the Shaker villages of Canterbury, New Hampshire, and Pleasant Hill (Harrodsburg), Kentucky, as well as the Hunt-Morgan house in Lexington, Kentucky. I also consulted the Abraham Lincoln Papers at the Library of Congress and received valuable help from the Shaker Historical Society in Shaker Heights, Ohio. Thanks also to Wendy Zarara, broomsquire (broom maker) at Hale Farm and Village in Bath, Ohio.

Duke, Basil W. *A History of Morgan's Cavalry*. First published 1867 by the author. Reprint edition, Centennial Civil War Series. Bloomington: Indiana University Press, 1960.

Folger, Randy. *Gentle Words: Shaker Music*. Cassette tape. Americana Productions, 1993.

Horwitz, Lester V. *The Longest Raid of the Civil War*. Cincinnati, Ohio: Farmcourt Publishing, 1999.

Murray, Stuart. *Shaker Heritage Guidebook: Exploring the Historic Sites, Museums and Collections*. Spencertown, N.Y.: Golden Hill Press, 1993.

Piercy, Caroline B. *The Shaker Cookbook: Not by Bread Alone*. New York: Crown Publishers, 14th printing, 1977.

Sprigg, June, and David Larkin. *Shaker: Life, Work, and Art*. New York: Smithmark Publishers, 1987.

Stein, Stephen J. *The Shaker Experience in America*. New Haven, Conn.: Yale University Press, 1992.

Thorne-Thomsen, Kathleen. *Shaker Children: True Stories and Crafts*. Chicago: Chicago Review Press, 1996.

Whiteley, Elder John, of Shirley Village, Massachusetts. *A Shaker's Answer to the Oft-Repeated Question, "What Would Become of the World If All Should Become Shakers?"* Boston: Press of Rand, Avery, & Co., 1874. Reprinted 1978.

Young, Mary Lawrence, and Bill Mastin. *The Pleasant Hill, Kentucky, Shakertown Coloring Book*. Self-published, 1997.